HOW TO KILL A
GIANT

ENDORSEMENTS

How to Kill a Giant will captivate middle-grade readers from the moment three discontented young adolescents begin searching a creepy old house for a missing pet cat until the inspiring conclusion of this wonderfully imaginative story. Hugo and two friends, siblings Julia and Stefan, discover a strange, ancient Bible. Then the three are miraculously transported to ancient Israel, where they meet the biblical hero David when he was a young shepherd. This tale gives new meaning to the Scripture that says the word of God is living and active. Carol Schlorff skillfully weaves a fast-moving story that teaches lessons of friendship, forgiveness, courage, and faith in God.

—Chuck Richardson, author of *True Status*

In *How to Kill a Giant*, Carol Schlorff brings a lively and creative perspective to an ancient story, reminding us that God is strong enough to fulfill His plans in our lives. As Hugo, Julia, and Stefan find out, in the middle of impossible circumstances, God is able to help us battle giants. Though each of our giants may look different, we can rely on God's strength as we trust Him to prepare us and lead us in the way we should go.

—Cynthia d'Entremont, author of *Simon Stayed, Oak Island Revenge*, and *Unlocked*

The author has crafted an adventure story packed with biblical truth relevant for today's kids. It teaches an age-old principle with the potential to change readers' lives: "Be of good courage" when facing giants of any description because God's presence gives strength and victory.

—Grace Fox, career missionary and award-winning author, *Moving from Fear to Freedom: A Woman's Guide to Peace in Every Situation*

HOW TO KILL A GIANT

How to Kill a Giant is an incredible middle grade novel that brings the Bible to life. Full of rich dialogue and vivid scenes, the characters learn about the life of David and the God he serves. If you ever wanted to get to know the lowly shepherd boy from Bethlehem, now is your chance. What a beautiful picture of the compassion and strength of God working in the hearts of young people. How to Kill a Giant is an adventurous book for young readers who love an action-packed story and practical ways to live out their faith in the real world.

—**Kim Patton**, author of *Nothing Wasted* (November 2023) and contributing writer for Shaunti Feldhahn and Waiting in Hope ministry

HOW TO KILL A
GIANT

CAROL SCHLORFF

ELK LAKE PUBLISHING INC

PUBLISHING THE POSITIVE
Plymouth, Massachusetts

A Christian Company
ElkLakePublishingInc.com

COPYRIGHT NOTICE

Cover and Interior Design: Kelly Artieri, Derinda Babcock, Deb Haggerty
Editor(s): Maria Riley, Deb Haggerty

PUBLISHED BY: Elk Lake Publishing, Inc., 35 Dogwood Drive, Plymouth, MA 02360, 2023

Library Cataloging Data
Names: Schlorff, Carol (Carol Schlorff)
How to Kill a Giant / Carol Schlorff

168 p. 23cm × 15cm (9in × 6 in.)
ISBN-13: 978-1-64949-916-5 (paperback) | 978-1-64949-917-2 (trade hardcover) | 978-1-64949-918-9 (trade paperback) | 978-1-64949-919-6 (e-book)
Key Words: teen novels on fear; young teen Christian novels; David and Goliath book; time-travel adventures; middle-grade Christian fiction; adventure novels for teens; biblical novels for teens

Library of Congress Control Number: 2023940835 Fiction

DEDICATION

To all who face a giant of fear.

ACKNOWLEDGMENTS

Writing may be a solitary endeavor, but no one turns the first draft into something acceptable for publication—much less publishes it—without the help of many. When I set out on the journey of writing my first novel, I had no idea what I was getting into. But the Lord placed people on my path every step of the way to help me move forward, and I would like to thank them publicly.

Grace Fox—for your advice, without which I wouldn't have even gotten off the ground.

Dorisa Costello—for your invaluable comments on my first draft and for not laughing so hard that I could hear you all the way to Cracow.

Bill Myers—for your critique that sent my manuscript in a new—and better—direction.

Christian Conway—for making sure my male characters were believable.

Makenna Linsky—for your insightful edits and input so that my teen protagonists were realistic.

Roksana Hybel, Veronika McCray, Pola Jasica—for giving me your teenage perspectives.

Maria Riley—for your edits and comments, which made my book much better than it was before.

Deb Haggerty—for taking a chance on me when no one else would.

And finally, I would like to thank my parents, Sam and Frederica Schlorff, for teaching me about Christ and showing me what it means to love and trust God. Thank you for patiently answering my countless questions about faith and helping me understand the reasons why. Without you, I would have never even come up with the idea for this book. And because of you, my passion is to show that the Bible is trustworthy and relevant today.

CHAPTER ONE

THE WORST SUMMER EVER

Hugo couldn't catch up to the shadowy figure in the distance, no matter how hard he tried. He ran over a rocky and uneven path, and the strange sandals on his feet made him lose his balance and sent him flying. Hugo hit the ground with a thud and lay motionless in pain and frustration. With all the strength he could muster, he jumped to his feet and scanned the hillside in every direction, but he was alone in this eerie wilderness and had no idea where to go. Panicked, he couldn't breathe, and his muscles shook.

Hugo's eyes sprang open, and he sat straight up. Disoriented, he looked around the room. *Oh, I'm home.* He collapsed back on his bed. His heart was pounding so fast he was sure it would break free from his rib cage at any moment. Every muscle in his body was taut. It had only been a nightmare, yet it had felt so real. He turned over on his side and tried to think of something else, but the image from the dream refused to fade. It was a long time before he fell back asleep.

When the sun shone brightly through his window shades, Hugo dragged himself to the kitchen. He poured a bowl of cereal and collapsed onto the chair, where he sat with his chin resting in his hands.

"Your cornflakes are getting soggy," Mom said as she walked by. Hugo shrugged and stared at his spoon laying on the table.

She paused to look at him. Her eyes revealed a deep sadness. "If there had been any other way—"

"Mom, please!"

She flinched at his outburst. A tear trickled down her cheek. "I can drop you off at the library on my way to work." She gave him a nervous smile.

"Sure. Whatever."

Hugo watched her disappear through the door. He ran his fingers through his dark, curly hair. The scene from his nightmare replayed over and over in his mind as he pondered what it meant. Then it hit him. *The dream represents my life,* he told himself. *I'm lost and alone.* He would have smiled at this discovery if only the last few months hadn't been so traumatic.

An hour later, Hugo entered the town library, his lone public hangout. Books and magazines were his faithful friends—his only friends. He hurried to his favorite spot, the lounge area full of sofas so soft you sank into them like quicksand. The room was more crowded than usual, with only one free couch. He sat down and scanned his magazine's table of contents when he spotted a boy and girl standing before him. They both had light brown hair and were the same height, but that's where the similarities ended. The boy was stocky with a square face, a flat nose, and short spiky hair, while the girl was slender with a round face and upturned nose, and her shoulder-length hair curled slightly at the ends.

Without warning, the girl plopped down on the far side of the sofa. "No one's sitting here, right." It wasn't a question.

Hugo didn't answer. He drew the publication closer to his face.

The boy settled in the space between them, and he and the girl pulled out their phones. No one said a word, but the boy continued to glance in Hugo's direction.

"My name's Stefan. What's yours?"

"What? Oh, er, I'm Hugo."

"And I'm Julia."

An awkward silence followed.

"My sister and I came here for the summer. We're staying with our grandparents."

Why do I need to know this? Hugo wondered. He stared down at the magazine but couldn't find the spot where he'd stopped reading.

"Can you tell us about your town?" The boy's big brown eyes sparkled at him.

"No," Hugo said abruptly. He realized his tone was rude, so he added, "I mean, I can't. I've only been living here for a few months." He gazed down at his feet, noticing a big stain on his left sneaker.

"How do you like it here?" Stefan asked.

Hugo thought about what to answer. He wasn't about to admit to the truth. The reality was he hated it. He had been horrified when his parents announced their move—on his thirteenth birthday, no less. They uprooted him from the only place he knew to come to live a thousand miles away in small-town Pennsylvania. He winced at the memory of his first day at school when his new classmates ignored him and the bullies marked him as an easy target. And then there was—*Nope. Not going there.* He shuddered.

"We don't like staying with Grandma and Grandpa either," Julia said.

"I didn't say I didn't like it." He grimaced, angry at himself for being so transparent.

"Do you have any brothers or sisters?" Stefan asked.

"No, I don't, but I have a dog."

"Really? We have a cat," Julia said. "What's your dog's name?"

They sure are nosy. Can't they mind their own business? Hugo muttered to himself, then suddenly remembered they were waiting for his answer. "Gibson."

A shared love for animals allowed their conversation to slowly pick up steam. The more they talked, the more convinced Hugo became that the siblings were hurting just as much as he was. An occasional word or facial expression betrayed the same confusion and sorrow he felt. He was sure they understood his pain. It turned out they were practically the same age—Julia was fourteen, and Stefan was twelve. When they discovered they were staying on Hugo's street, the siblings invited him over.

The day of his visit finally arrived, but Hugo was nervous. What if they rejected him too? When he saw their house, his heart skipped a beat. It was an imposing old brick and stone structure that looked down on the rest of the street from its high perch on a hill. Hugo almost did an about-face, but his parents would be disappointed if he did. He approached the front door and hesitated for a full minute before ringing the bell.

"Hi! Come in." Julia greeted him with a friendly grin.

"Hey!" He smiled back. He stepped inside and looked around the large hall. It was like being in a museum with antique furniture and impressive paintings everywhere in sight.

"How *old* is this house?" he couldn't keep from asking, then felt stupid for doing so and winced.

"I don't know—over a hundred years for sure."

Hugo wondered what secrets and mysteries the walls would share if they could speak as he followed Julia down the corridor.

He was about to take a step, but his foot froze in mid-air. He brought his leg down and backed up, almost tripping over himself. The largest cat he had ever seen had stepped into the hallway. The beast was nearly the size of a cocker spaniel.

"It's—huge!" He pointed to the animal staring at him with big green eyes. "Is that a bobcat?"

"Don't be silly. His name is Domino. He's a Maine Coon." She noticed Hugo's blank stare. "They're the largest breed of cats."

The boy didn't move. Domino had gray fur mixed with swirls of red, topped off with a white patch on his nose, neck, and belly. He strolled towards Hugo.

"Is he friendly?"

Julia laughed. "Of course he is."

Hugo wasn't so sure and eyed the approaching animal with growing dread. Julia knelt next to Domino, who dropped down on the floor, stretched out onto his side, and meowed.

"See, he wants to be petted." She stroked his soft fur. "Come here."

"I can't. I'm allergic," he lied. He felt a pang of guilt but would never admit to being afraid of a cat. Taking a step back, he hit the wall and almost knocked over one of the paintings. He caught it in time and quickly looked at Julia, still stroking Domino. Whew! She hadn't noticed. He wiped the sweat that had formed on his brow.

Julia stood up and signaled for him to follow. He went out of his way to avoid the cat still lying on the floor. They came to a large living room. It had the same museum-like feel.

When Stefan saw them, he jumped up from his chair to rush in their direction. "Can you believe there's no Wi-Fi?" He held out his useless smartphone as proof.

Hugo was shocked. "What do you mean? How can you survive?"

"Oh, there's the internet, all right," Julia said. "Grandma and Grandpa don't want Wi-Fi for health reasons." She rolled her eyes.

"I guess you don't have it so bad, then."

"Oh, we do!" Stefan stomped his foot. "Their computers are so old I can't play any of my games." He gave Hugo a look as if to say, "See what we have to suffer."

"How long will you be here?"

Julia and Stefan's countenances darkened. They stared at each other for a few seconds before turning back towards Hugo, who thought he could see tears in Julia's eyes.

"We don't know," she muttered. "Whenever Mom and Dad come back for us." Her shoulders sagged, and she threw herself on the couch.

Hugo felt terrible seeing how sad she looked but decided against asking for more details. No one said a word for so long that Hugo felt uncomfortable. Mercifully, the door opened, and the siblings' grandparents entered the room.

"You must be Hugo," Grandma said. She was a petite woman with wavy brown hair without a speck of gray. "Welcome, and make yourself at home." Her eyes shone with kindness. "Come into the kitchen. I have some goodies waiting for you."

Hugo and the siblings hurried after her.

He was hiking along a rocky path in the wilderness, wearing those same weird sandals, when a towering hulk of a man suddenly appeared before him. His features were mostly hidden—like in a picture out of focus—except for his bulging biceps. An overwhelming terror took hold of Hugo, who sprinted in the opposite direction, but he felt powerful hands grab him from behind and lift him straight off his feet. He tried to shake loose, but the man's grip was too firm. He screamed but instinctively knew no one could hear him.

Hugo woke up. He lay in bed, sweat pouring down his face—another nightmare. While his pulse slowly returned to normal, his distress refused to let go. Both dreams had been so vivid and with the same strange sandals! What could they mean? He was sure they contained a message he couldn't decipher. Maybe this new nightmare was his mind's sick way of rehashing his encounters with the bullies and *the day*. Or perhaps the dreams were a warning about something else altogether. He fell back into a troubled sleep.

He overslept, then rushed to eat breakfast and to visit Julia and Stefan. By now, he knew every detail of the way by heart. Their house had become his main hangout these last two weeks.

The sky looked innocent enough when he waved goodbye to his mom, but in record time, a thick layer of clouds rolled in and dumped its contents on Hugo. He sprinted to the house and knocked. Julia threw the door open.

"Hey!" he mumbled as he rushed inside. "It's bad out there. So much for going to the woods today," he shivered.

They had planned to go to a nearby forest where they sometimes explored or took pictures of plants and insects. Their phones' cameras and features allowed them to experiment for hours to get the best shots and effects until the batteries ran out.

Hugo followed Julia to the living room and sank into a couch. She sat beside him and looked up as Stefan marched into the room.

"What are we going to do now?" Stefan asked. He threw himself on a chair. "I'm bored already!"

Julia looked up at the ceiling and huffed. "Stop complaining, will you?"

"You can't tell me what to do." He stuck out his tongue at her.

Julia's nostrils flared, and with a sweeping gesture, she crossed her arms and turned her back to her brother.

Hugo couldn't think of a way to defuse the situation. His mind felt like a hard drive that had frozen up. After a few seconds, his brain rebooted. "Let's go to the library."

Julia didn't say a word.

Stefan shook his head. "Grandma and Grandpa have gone to the doctor. We're stuck." He leaned forward to cradle his head in his hands. "This is the worst summer ever!"

Not only the summer. Hugo bit his lip.

Julia straightened up. "Let's play Monopoly," she proclaimed.

Stefan jumped up to get the game. "It's my turn to win."

"Says who?" Julia turned towards Hugo. "You two won't stand a chance."

Hugo smirked but didn't say a word. He knew board games weren't exactly her strength. She lacked any visible strategy. On the other hand, he was a thinker, always planning his moves. There was the unfortunate factor of chance to consider, and because of pure luck—as he saw it—Julia had won once or twice. As for Stefan, he wasn't a threat whatsoever. He was too impulsive and acted without forethought. Even luck couldn't help him.

Before long, the board game was on the table, and they were deep into buying and selling. Things weren't going as Hugo had anticipated. To his growing surprise and irritation, Stefan was accumulating properties, hotels, and money.

"Not again!" Julia exclaimed when she landed on her brother's real estate. "I don't think I have enough to pay you. How about a discount?" She batted her eyelashes at him.

"Are you kidding?" He stretched his hand towards her, palm facing up, and shot her a smug look.

She hesitated before giving him all she had.

Stefan laughed as he took the money. "I knew I'd win. You're such a lousy player."

Julia didn't respond, but her mood was worsening by the second. When the game ended, which mercifully didn't take long, Julia was in full sulk mode. She thrust out her lower lip, retreated to the couch, and theatrically turned away from the boys with a flounce, refusing to speak.

"She's such a sore loser," Stefan said to Hugo. He looked over at his sister. "You're acting just like Mom when she's fighting with Dad."

Julia whipped around to stare at her brother, both eyes and mouth wide open. She fought to hold back the tears. Hugo could feel her hurt from across the room.

No one spoke. The siblings sat with their arms crossed, glaring at the floor. Hugo was surprised at Stefan's comment since they had never mentioned any family discord. Then again, he hadn't been very forthcoming about his problems at school either.

The silence lasted for about five minutes when a loud bang from upstairs made them jump.

CHAPTER TWO

WHERE'S DOMINO?

"What was that noise?" Julia sat up straight, her pouting instantly forgotten.

"Maybe Domino knocked something over," Hugo said.

"I don't think so," she replied. "It sounded much too loud, like a door slamming shut."

"But there's no one else here," Stefan said.

"Someone could have snuck in unnoticed. I told Grandma and Grandpa to lock the back door! But *no*, they can't find the key." Her eyes grew big. "Maybe a burglar is searching the house!"

Hugo's imagination took off with the worst possible scenarios. What if an escaped convict was hiding upstairs, or even worse, a serial killer?

"Man, I really wish we weren't alone," Julia whispered.

Nobody moved, too scared to do anything. They waited for a few minutes, but they only heard the sound of their own breathing. Eventually, they decided to investigate and slowly tiptoed up the steps.

They came to a large hallway, which was wide at first and then narrowed halfway down. It plunged into semi-darkness that the ceiling lights couldn't entirely dispel. The three looked around cautiously. Empty. Bedrooms lined both sides of the corridor and at the very end was a dark and solitary door leading to the attic. Hugo wondered what creepy creatures could be hiding up in the dark.

He had never been invited upstairs before, but he could now understand why—this floor was spooky. A chill ran up and down his back. He had the impression something terrifying could jump out of a door at any moment.

They crept into the first bedroom on the right. Two single beds lined the wall with a window between them, and a large dresser stood on the opposite side.

"This is where we're sleeping," Julia whispered.

"You're sharing a room?" Hugo raised an eyebrow. Julia and Stefan looked at each other, then lowered their eyes.

"We're afraid of being alone," Julia said in a hushed tone.

Hugo looked around the room. "I can understand why." He could almost feel the shadows gathering in every corner. "This floor gives me the creeps."

"You too?" Stefan asked.

They snuck up to the closet. Hugo grabbed the doorknob and threw it open on the count of three. Holding their breath, the siblings poked their heads inside. Empty.

They inched their way down the daunting hallway and examined every room, including the attic. Fortunately, no burglar was in sight.

"No one's here." Hugo felt his muscles relax. "The house has got to be empty!"

"What caused that sound, then?" Julia said.

"As I said, Domino probably knocked something over."

"I don't think so. We would have found whatever he broke. And by the way, where is he?" She turned toward Stefan. "Did you notice him anywhere?"

Her brother shook his head.

Perplexed, Julia scanned the corridor as a faint sound reached their ears.

It took a few seconds to recognize what they were hearing. It was a meow. And it sounded like a distress signal.

"He must be hurt!" Julia dashed into the first room, the boys right behind her.

No cat was to be found anywhere, not under the bed or in the closet. There was also complete silence. Puzzled, the three returned to the hallway and perked up their ears. The faint meow resumed. They hurried into the next room and searched every nook and cranny to no avail. There was no sound, either. Back in the hallway, they heard Domino again.

They repeated this process with every room, but the meowing stopped when they left the hall, only to resume when they returned to the corridor.

"Where could he be?" Julia shrieked, her voice two octaves higher than usual. She reached up her hand to twirl the ends of her hair with a vengeance. "How strange. We hear him in the hallway but not in the bedrooms."

Hugo frowned. "It sounds as if he's in one of the walls."

"What?" Julia's body shook.

"He'll be fine unless—" Hugo clamped his mouth shut.

"Unless what?" She gave him a desperate look.

"Unless—he runs out of air."

Stefan and Julia gasped. Hugo felt guilty for adding more distress to an already tense situation. He had to do something, so he motioned for them to be quiet and slowly paced the corridor. When he returned, he hesitated to say what was on his mind.

"Have you noticed anything?" Julia asked.

"I'm not sure."

"If you have an idea, spit it out!" she ordered. "Domino's life is on the line."

Hugo scratched the back of his neck. "I think he's a little louder here." He pointed to where a picture hung on the wall. An idea barged into his mind. *Could it be?* "Don't move. I need to check something out." He disappeared into one of the rooms, only to quickly return and enter the adjacent one. When he reemerged, he was confident his theory was correct. "It looks like these two rooms don't touch. There's some space between them, exactly where the meowing is somewhat louder."

"You mean like a secret room? Awesome!" Stefan's eyes glowed with excitement.

"Maybe. I think the first room ends where that picture is, but the next one ends here." He walked over to a spot about five feet from the painting. "There could be a hidden closet of some kind, but how did Domino get in?"

"There's got to be a secret door!" Stefan slapped the wall with his hand. "Who knows, it could have an old treasure no one knows about. It could be worth millions!"

"Or maybe someone was murdered," Julia said, "and they put the body in there and covered up the entrance. The poor victim could be a skeleton by now."

"I think both of you have seen way too many movies," Hugo smirked. "But, if we don't find a way to get in there soon, Domino will become a skeleton himself." Hugo immediately regretted his words when Julia and Stefan flinched and looked at him with despair.

After a few moments of indecision, they decided to pat down every inch of the wall in the hallway in hopes of finding a secret door. Nothing was out of the ordinary.

Disheartened, they entered the bedroom where Julia and Stefan were staying. They went past Julia's bed to the wall adjacent to the mysterious secret space and touched every square inch to no avail.

"To think there could be a body there, and I've been sleeping so close to it." She shrunk back.

"There's no dead body anywhere," Hugo said. He stomped his foot. He didn't want to hear her ridiculous theories which only fed his own fears.

"How do you know?"

There was a short pause. "Okay, so I don't know for sure. It's probably a long-lost closet full of cleaning supplies."

"Let's check the other room." Julia dashed into the hallways with the boys right behind her. The meowing had stopped.

"Oh no, he's dead!" she cried out. "Domino! Domino!" She ran towards the spot where he had been the loudest. The faint meowing started up again. She looked over at the boys, beaming. "He's alive!"

They rushed into the next room, which was small and appeared to have once been a study. The only furniture was a chair, some built-in shelves as ancient as the house itself, and an old drop-front secretary desk overflowing with papers and documents.

Four large framed wooden panels, each engraved with various animals, covered the wall next to the secret place.

"Don't you see?" Hugo's eyes sparkled. "One of these panels could be a door. It would make a perfect hidden entrance."

"You're right!" Julia squealed. She approached the dark wood and ran her fingers over a carved deer. "I bet this was made when they built the house. It's beautiful."

Stefan marched up to the panels, placed both hands around the edges, then pulled hard to see if they would budge, but the paneling stayed firmly in place.

"Be careful! We don't want to damage them." Julia scowled.

"I'm just trying to help."

Hugo laughed. "I doubt Domino used brute force." He inspected the room. "So, how *did* he get in?"

Something caught Hugo's attention, something on the lowest shelf on the wall. He leaned forward to study it. Each end had a tiny metal figurine of a cat. *How ironic!*

The one on the right wasn't standing up straight. Instead, it tilted to the left, like a clock needle pointing at 10 o'clock. How could it stay put without falling over? Hugo reached out to pick the cat up, but it was attached to something and wouldn't budge. He pushed it, causing the small figurine to move to the right and stand up straight. Nothing happened. He tilted it again to the left.

The loud screech made everyone jolt. The three looked on in fascination as one of the panels began to move. Hugo had found the trigger! The mechanism groaned and hissed loudly while the opening slowly grew wider.

Suddenly, a flash of fur came bursting out of the darkness. It was so quick and unexpected that Julia screamed, Stefan jumped, and Hugo leapt back, banging into the wall. *Ouch!* When they realized what it was, they let out a shout of joy.

"Domino!" Julia swept the cat into her arms, hugging him tightly. He showed his disapproval by clawing at her arm with his only free paw. Julia let him go, and he rubbed up against her and purred.

They turned their attention to the secret opening. Hugo's mouth went dry, and scenes from the few scary movies he had seen flashed across his mind, causing him to imagine a monster or ghost bursting out from the darkness. *Snap out of it! Don't be such a wimp.* He jerked his head from side to side to scrap the image from his mind.

The three kids stared at the door, unsure what to do next. Suddenly, it slammed shut with a loud bang, causing everyone to jump. Domino almost hit the ceiling, and the others weren't far behind.

"That's what caused the noise we heard! Let's open it again and see what's inside!" Stefan shouted. He bolted towards the shelf and shifted the cat figurine as Hugo had. Sure enough, the door moved again.

"We better prop it open this time. We don't want to be stuck inside, do we?" Hugo said.

The siblings gave him a horrified look. All three hurried to the desk and dragged it to the door with great difficulty, leaving a trail of papers on the floor behind them.

"There's no way the door will close now," Hugo said, "but let's wait to make sure, just in case."

They watched the paneling while the seconds ticked away at a painfully slow pace, but finally, the mechanism gave way. The door slammed into the desk, which held its ground, but the jolt sent more papers flying across the room.

The dark opening stood before them. The three kids shuffled closer. The area beyond was so pitch black they couldn't see a thing. They looked for a light switch but couldn't find any.

"I'm not going in there without knowing what's inside first." Julia backed away. "I don't want to bump into some skeleton or dead body that's been mummifying for a hundred years."

"Will you cut it out with your dead bodies!" Hugo's imagination was already running wild and didn't need any help.

"We need a flashlight." Julia moved towards the door. "I left my phone downstairs. I'll get it. You two can stay here."

The boys glanced at each other. "We're coming with you," they both said almost simultaneously and rushed to follow her.

As they scurried down the hall, Hugo spotted a camping lantern in a corner by the stairs. "Look, this lamp will work." He pointed, and Julia grabbed it. They dashed back to the room.

"You go first!" Julia handed Hugo the lantern and pushed him forward.

"Why me?" He backed away from her. "Maybe, Stefan, you want to have the honors?"

But the boy just gaped at him, slowly shaking his head.

Hugo felt as if his feet were glued to the floor. His body refused to cooperate even as he tried to muster enough courage to take a step forward.

After a few seconds, Julia huffed and snatched the lantern from his hands. She took a shaky step towards the dark opening. Her hands trembled as she held the lantern as far forward as possible. The light gradually illuminated the secret room, falling on a chair and a table. No dead bodies in sight. Julia took a deep breath, crawled under the desk, and stepped inside the room. She lifted the lantern so its light shone brightly in the cramped space.

The only furniture was the chair and narrow table. All the walls were covered with handwritten notes on yellowing paper held in place by nails. Julia hung the lantern on one of them, first making sure it was strong enough to hold it up.

The boys followed Julia inside and surveyed the small room in silence. Strangely, Hugo felt like they were trespassing on someone's private space. He had the weird impression they were standing on holy ground and should show the appropriate respect.

"Look at all these notes!" Julia whispered. "What do they say?"

The walls were full of quotes written in old English, with "Thee's" and "Thou's" and many incomprehensible words. Everything was written in beautiful cursive. Hugo leaned forward to examine the writing more carefully. *No one writes like this anymore.* Much of the ink had faded, but the beauty of the letters enthralled him nonetheless. The handwriting was the same everywhere, as if one person had written it all.

One note caught Julia's attention. "Huh, easier said than done," she whispered.

"What do you mean?" Hugo turned towards her.

She hesitated, then pointed to a quote with larger letters than the rest. She read, "It says, 'Be of good courage.' Whoever wrote this has never been in my family," she mumbled.

Hugo reread the words. *Whoever wrote this has never been to my school.*

Their attention turned to the table. It was empty except for a large leather-bound book, almost the size of an Xbox One. Like everything else in the room, it was very old—maybe even older than the house itself. Someone had used it a lot. The spine had begun to separate, and a few loose pages were sticking out from the side. The cover was well-worn, and a large cross was carved into the dark brown leather. The book was so perfectly in the center of the table that somebody must have lovingly cared for it.

The three stared at it for a moment, not daring to touch it, when Stefan abruptly reached down and turned over the front cover, causing a little cloud of dust to float across the room.

"Be careful with it!" Julia whispered. She grabbed his hand and jerked it aside. "Can't you see it's falling apart?"

"Why are you whispering? Are you afraid someone might hear us?" Stefan spoke straight into her ear.

Julia stared at him, dumbfounded. "I—I don't know why. It just seems appropriate." She leaned closer to the open book. A name was written in bold and beautiful letters on the top of the page, "Anna Maria." The handwriting matched the quotes on the walls.

"Anna Maria? Wasn't there an Anna Maria back in our family?" Julia asked, this time in a normal tone. "Some great-great-great-grandmother or something?"

"I don't know." Stefan shrugged. "Family stuff never interested me."

"The name rings a bell." Julia scrunched her face. "I know! I think she and her husband built this house!" Stefan gave his sister a blank stare.

They looked further down the page. The words "Holy Bible" were printed in beautiful calligraphy. Underneath was a handwritten note: "May blessings fall on anyone who reads this hallowed book. May the words contained within come alive and change heart and soul. May the reader experience truth and come away forever changed. Amen."

"How can the words come alive?" Stefan asked. The other two just blinked back at him.

"This room is so strange. It's as if someone came here to read the Bible, but why?" Julia looked around again.

Hugo chuckled. "Good question. Why would anyone want to?"

"Why not?" Julia turned towards him.

"Well, er, it's boring, isn't it?"

"Have you ever read it?" she inquired.

"Um, no," Hugo answered sheepishly.

"So, how do you know it's boring?" She crossed her arms with a smug expression on her face.

Hugo didn't have an answer. "What about you? Have you read it?"

"No, but at least I don't go around giving my opinion about things I know nothing about."

"Really?" Stefan grabbed his heart and staggered backward.

His sister gave him a dirty look. "Like you know so much about it." She then turned her attention back to the table. The boys stood on either side of her looking at the old book.

Julia carefully turned over a few pages, and the lifelike illustrations enthralled all three of them. The drawings of serpents, soldiers, and kings almost jumped off the pages. They came to a simple picture of a young shepherd surrounded by his sheep and paused. The love in the boy's eyes was so real they couldn't stop staring at him.

"I wonder who he is," Julia said. "Look how much he cares for his sheep."

They continued to gaze at the image when something strange happened. The animals moved. It was barely noticeable at first, but after a few seconds, Hugo had no doubt—the heads were nodding up and down, and the hoofs were clopping back and forth.

Hugo glanced in shock at the siblings, whose puzzled gaze reflected back at him. Suddenly, the room began to swerve as if they were in a boat during a storm. Hugo lost his balance and went crashing to the floor. Stefan landed on top of him and quickly rolled off while Julia hit the table.

The sheep were soon in the room with them, bleating wildly. At the sight of them, Hugo's heart started racing so quickly he was sure it would explode—just as he had felt on *the day*. Everything spun faster and faster, accompanied by an earsplitting roar. Hugo pressed his hands over his ears, and everything went black.

CHAPTER THREE

A Weird Shepherd in a Strange Land

Hugo opened a sleepy eye. At first, he thought he was at home, but what he was lying on was much too hard to be his bed, and the light was much too bright to be his room. He looked up and saw nothing but blue sky. *Strange.* He slowly stirred to life. *Where am I?* He looked around, and the shock of what he saw jolted him out of his dreamy state. He hopped to his feet.

He was on the side of a ridge. He looked in every direction, but the view was the same as far as he could see. The terrain was hilly and arid with rocks, gnarled trees, and measly shrubs sprinkled around. The area was covered with green grass which had turned brown in spots, creating the semblance of a two-colored carpet.

The sun was shining brightly without a cloud in the sky. The weirdest thing of all wasn't the landscape—it was his clothes. Gone were his jeans and T-shirt. Instead, he wore a beige knee-length wool tunic with a leather belt around his waist and leather sandals. He felt a chill when he recognized them from his dreams. Over everything was a woolen cloak, which reminded him of a poncho. The rough and uncomfortable cloth itched his body all over.

I'm back in my nightmare, but it's even more real. He turned around, and his heart skipped a beat. Stefan and

Julia were sleeping on the ground a few feet away. They were dressed as strangely as he was, except Julia's tunic reached her ankles, and a shawl covered her hair. An uncontrollable sense of panic rose within him. Hugo shook so violently that he had to sit back down to avoid falling. He tried uselessly to rein his emotions back under control. A long time went by before the trembling stopped. He had no idea what to think.

Julia stirred first. She looked up at him and then at her surroundings. She felt for the shawl, trying to figure out what was on her head. Dumfounded, she yelled for Stefan to get up. He opened one eye at a time and surveyed the landscape. He then sat up with a start, mouth gaping open.

Why am I not waking up?

"Where are we?" Stefan asked. "What are these clothes?" He cautiously patted his cloak as if it would give him an electric shock.

Julia tried to twirl her hair, but her shawl got in the way.

Hugo looked at the siblings, and a realization made his blood turn to ice. *I'm not in a dream. This is real.*

"Did we die and go to heaven?" Stefan asked.

"At this point, I'm not ruling anything out," Hugo answered, scanning the horizon. "I don't think heaven looks like this." He put his hand on his chest. "We're breathing, so we must be alive. Dead people don't breathe." He pinched himself. "And they don't feel pain, either."

"The last thing I remember was being in the secret room and looking at the old Bible," Julia said, "then we woke up here. Could the two be related?"

"I doubt it. How could they be?" Hugo replied.

They stood up but didn't know what to do next. Which way should they go? Every direction looked the same.

They heard some movement nearby. Someone was coming their way! Alarmed, they looked around for a hiding place and fell to the ground behind a scraggly bush.

A lone sheep came into view. It was strolling and stopped to nibble at the grass. Before long, several other sheep joined it, then more followed behind, including some little lambs staying close to their mothers. The animals grazed peacefully, unaware of the children hiding behind the bush.

Without warning, Stefan laughed and stood up, startling the sheep. They scurried away from him, bleating nervously.

In a flash, a young man appeared out of nowhere, his dark eyes burning with rage. He sprinted up to Stefan and lifted what looked like a policeman's club, bringing it within an inch of the boy's head.

"Who are you? What are you doing here?" he questioned. "Just try stealing one of my sheep, and you'll regret it for the rest of your life!" His eyes narrowed. "If you live."

Stefan's jaw dropped open. He stood stock-still, unable to answer.

The shepherd looked behind the boy. "The two of you hiding can get up now." He kept his club pointed at Stefan's head until Julia and Hugo obeyed. He then lowered his arm and glared at them. No one spoke.

"I asked you a question." He scowled at Stefan.

Julia stepped forward. "Um, my name is Julia. This is Stefan, my brother, and our friend Hugo." Silence followed while the young man and the three assessed each other.

"And what's your name?" Stefan asked once he regained his composure.

"I'm David," the shepherd said.

He was older than they were, about seventeen or eighteen. He was only slightly taller than Hugo, sported thick shoulder-length reddish-brown hair, and was as good-looking as a movie star. Although his frame was somewhat thin, he was intimidating, nonetheless. His clothes matched theirs, and his cloak was covered in dirt. It probably hadn't seen a washing machine in a while.

"Your names are weird. What tribe are you from?"

They stared at him with blank expressions on their faces.

"We're from Pennsyl—" Stefan said, but Hugo's piercing look caused him to stop mid-sentence. This time, it was David's turn to gawk at them without understanding.

There was a long pause. Hugo didn't know why, but he had a feeling the less they said about themselves, the better.

Julia again bravely broke the silence. "Where are we?"

David did a double take, and then frowned. "You're in the hill country of Judah."

"What's Judah?" Stefan asked.

David gaped at them as if they had just fallen from the moon. His glare intensified. "Why exactly are you here?"

David was tensing up. Hugo feared if he didn't act soon, the shepherd might do something painful, but what could he say? How could he explain the truth? And frankly, what had happened? How did they end up in this place? Finally, he decided the best solution was to be as straightforward as possible.

"To be honest, we don't know how we got here," he said. Then an idea came to him. "We had an accident and have lost our memories."

David studied them long and hard. "But you know your names."

Hugo stood in silence while he quickly thought about how to answer. "Yes, we remember our names, but not much else." Hugo shifted back and forth, uncomfortable under the shepherd's stare. "We have no idea how we got here or where we want to go."

"What kind of accident did you have?" David's expression made it clear he wasn't buying their story.

26

"I wish I knew," Hugo answered with more emotion than he wanted.

The shepherd paced back and forth, deep in thought. "You're coming with me!" he snapped. "I want to keep an eye on you." His countenance made a chill slither up and down Hugo's spine.

"You'll stay the night with me, and then we'll see," David added without enthusiasm.

Julia, Stefan, and Hugo's eyes grew big. What did he mean by "we'll see?"

David bellowed a strange call, and the sheep came running from all the directions where they had scattered to graze. They surrounded him and pressed up against his body. He slowly counted them and, satisfied all were present, set out. With each step, David gradually made his way to the back of the flock, keeping a close eye on them to ensure the animals stayed together. Whenever one strayed, he slung a small stone in its direction so quickly and precisely that both Julia and Stefan flinched the first time it happened. The pebble always landed in the exact path of the wandering sheep, startling it and causing it to change direction and return to the others.

They walked in silence for what Hugo guessed was about fifteen minutes until they came to a high rock wall that formed a semicircle pressed up against a cliff. A narrow entryway was the only way in and out. Thorn bushes as sharp as barbed wire covered the top of the wall, and Hugo figured one careless move could cause a gash so deep it would require stitches.

The sheep entered one by one, bleating their contentment at being home. David waited until every animal was safe before motioning for his guests to go in, and he came last. He moved a large rock into the entryway.

"Welcome to my home," he said, but his eyes had a coldness that didn't match his words.

Hugo looked around with dismay at the spacious courtyard where he stood and the dark entrance to a cave on the side of the cliff. *This is where he lives? There's nothing here.* There was no furniture, only the hard ground. He searched without success for any sign of electricity or technology. *He has to have a cell phone around here somewhere. When I find it, I'll call Mom and Dad.* He frowned. *How can anyone live like this?* He glanced at the cave entrance. *Maybe it's all in there.*

He suddenly realized he badly needed to go to the bathroom. The siblings must have felt the same because, after a few uncomfortable moments, he heard the question he had been too embarrassed to ask.

"Where's the bathroom?" Stefan asked.

He got a vacant stare in return. "What's that?"

All three mouths dropped open. Hugo couldn't believe what he was hearing.

"Um, I need to pee. Where's the toilet? Or should I use the nearest rock?" Stefan gave David a look as if to say, "duh!"

The shepherd's eyes almost bulged out of their sockets. "What do you mean? You need me to tell you?"

Another long pause. Hugo furiously tried to come up with something to say. "I know it's crazy, but we've even forgotten how to—do the most basic functions." He winced inwardly at how stupid his words sounded. "We're helpless. We don't know anything." He had never felt more foolish!

David skeptically examined each of them. He finally gave them instructions while shaking his head in disbelief.

Julia gasped in horror at the shepherd's directions, and Hugo felt sorry for her. *Poor Julia. This is worse than even a port-o-potty.*

Hugo desperately wanted to talk to the siblings in private. They had to come up with a unified story to answer any questions the shepherd might have. He could tell David suspected them of something, and he was afraid the shepherd might turn them over to whatever authorities this country had. Or worse. He wished he could figure out what had happened. Where were they? Could they have been kidnapped? Was David in on the plot? But why would anyone want to take them captive?

After each of them attended to their business, one after the other, David began inspecting the sheep. Stefan followed him, curious at his every move. Although irritated by the attention, the shepherd politely answered his questions. Hugo's ears perked up as he nervously monitored Stefan's every word.

"What are you doing?"

"I'm checking to ensure she hasn't hurt herself or gotten ill."

David opened a tiny flask and rubbed oil on the head and nose of the sheep.

"What's the oil for?" Stefan inquired.

"It's to keep bugs away. Otherwise, the larvae will crawl up their nose and into their brain."

"Ew, gross!"

David gave him the satisfied smile of an older brother who had succeeded in repulsing a younger sibling.

"Are you always out with the sheep?"

"No, I'm sometimes called back to serve King Saul. I'm one of his armor-bearers," the shepherd replied.

Stefan's eyes widened. Hugo looked at Julia. *What did he say?*

"You have a king? Cool! What's an armor-bearer?" Stefan asked.

David stopped examining the sheep and fixed his gaze on the boy, dumbfounded. "I'm responsible for the king's weapons. Everyone knows about King Saul!" he replied, "even our enemies, the Philistines." He glared at Stefan, then resumed his inspection.

"Do you have a cell phone we could use?" Stefan continued, unabashed.

"What? Is it something you sit on? I only have sheepskins."

Before the stunned boy could answer, Hugo jumped in. "Yes, something similar." He turned towards Stefan with his back to the shepherd and mouthed, "drop it!" *So much for calling for help. I guess there's no internet, either.* His heart sank.

"Which reminds me, where are my manners?" David vanished into the cave and returned with four sheepskins, which he threw in a circle on the ground. "Please, sit down."

The three hesitated. *You expect us to sit on those things?*

When Hugo noticed David tapping his foot, he quickly obeyed, and the siblings followed suit. The sheepskins had an unpleasant odor. Julia wiggled her nose, Stefan unceremoniously pinched his nostrils between his thumb and finger, while Hugo chose to ignore the stench.

David was able to inspect his flock in peace for a few minutes. Unfortunately, Stefan was soon back at the shepherd's side, ogling his every move.

"Are you still going to school?" Stefan asked.

"What do you mean by school?"

Stefan almost choked on his saliva. "This is the ultimate paradise if you have no schools!" When he noticed the shepherd's confused expression, he continued. "It's a building where you go to learn. I don't like school. It's boring."

David cocked his head to one side and scrutinized the younger boy. "Well, I did have to study all about the Law. All boys attend classes, but unlike you, I enjoyed it." He gave Stefan a look of superiority.

"Do you like taking care of the sheep?"

David was taken aback by the question. "It's not important what I like. It's my job. I'm the youngest son, so it's my responsibility." He looked over at the animals, and his expression softened. "But I do love being with the sheep. They accept me as I am, don't argue back, and are happy to see me." He turned and walked away. "I can't say the same about most people," he mumbled. David headed to the other side of the courtyard as if trying to end the conversation, but Stefan trailed behind.

Julia spoke to her brother. "Stop asking so many questions. Don't you see he's tired of it?" She gave him a stern look. He stuck up his nose at her.

The shepherd glanced at the girl with gratitude and continued checking his flock in peace, but not for long.

"Do the sheep have names?" Stefan said.

"No, they don't."

"Why not? My cat's name is Domino."

"They're not pets."

"I would still give them names."

"Let me put it this way. If you have lamb for dinner, you probably don't want to think to yourself, *I'm eating Curly now.*" He glared at him. "Am I right?"

"Oh!" Stefan said, understanding dawning across his face.

"But," David continued, "You could say this one here almost has a name. She's the most hardheaded and rebellious sheep I've ever had. To make matters worse, she's unusually tall and strong. So whenever I look at her, the word 'trouble' comes to mind." He nodded toward the animal he was currently inspecting. Sure enough, she was fighting hard against his hold.

Convinced she was okay, he let her go, and she dashed away. He turned his attention to another sheep.

"Mom and Dad used to say my middle name was 'Trouble,'" Stefan blurted out.

"I can believe that!" David laughed.

Stefan scowled. He brusquely reached out to pet one of the animals, which sprinted away and caused others nearby to bolt.

"Sheep are easily scared, and if one panics, the others follow," David said. He took a deep breath and blew out the air. "So be careful not to frighten them, okay?"

"Of course!" all three kids answered in unison.

"Haven't you ever been with sheep before?" the shepherd muttered. "Or is it an act?" he whispered, and his eyes narrowed. David disappeared into the cave and returned carrying several large leather pouches. He sat down on one of the sheepskins.

"Time to eat," he said. "It's a good thing I just got resupplied by Father. Otherwise, there wouldn't be enough for the four of us."

At the mention of food, Hugo realized he was famished. His mind wandered to what he had eaten on camping trips. He thought of such delicious fare as grilled hotdogs, campfire macaroni and cheese, foil-wrapped roasted potatoes with all the trimmings, and sticky s'mores. Maybe David would offer them something similar?

David unrolled a leather covering and laid it on the ground like a blanket for a picnic. He then opened the pouches to expose their content. Hugo's pleasant anticipation turned to shock.

The first thing he noticed was something dark and thin. On closer inspection, it looked like fish someone had forgotten in the oven and burned to a crisp. Hugo almost gagged. The next bag contained a substance like cottage cheese but had a strong unpleasant smell. Other menu items included a thick tortilla, dried fruit resembling giant flattened raisins with little handles, and the plumpest and greenest olives Hugo had ever seen. The boy was horrified.

What kind of a joke is this? He can't be serious.

David prayed. "Blessed are you, O Lord our God, King of the world, who causes bread to come forth from the earth."

The siblings gave Hugo an incredulous stare. David, whose eyes were closed, didn't notice. He paused for a second and then turned towards his guests.

"Dig in!"

No one moved. The food looked disgusting, and Hugo and the siblings had no idea what to do. There were no forks, spoons, other utensils, or dishes. After a few minutes, David grew tired of waiting for them and helped himself to the food.

"Don't you have anything to make hamburgers?" Stefan asked, wrinkling his nose.

David stopped eating. "What are you talking about?"

The three jerked their heads to gawk at the shepherd. *Who doesn't know what a hamburger is?*

"It's a beef patty you eat on a bun with ketchup, lettuce, and tomato," Stefan explained. With his hands, he simulated making a hamburger and eating it.

David scowled. "Is that a Philistine dish?"

"No, it isn't." Hugo had no idea what he had denied, but the shepherd's ice-cold tone and fierce, unblinking stare were enough for him to know he better do so.

Hugo was desperate to diffuse the rising tension. Not knowing what else to do, he took a piece of the tortilla-looking thing, dipped it in the cheese as David had done, placed a few olives on top—one of which promptly rolled off—and, bracing himself for something nasty, shoved it into his mouth.

Wow! This food is good! He had never tasted anything so delicious. He took a few more bites before he got over his shock. He motioned for the siblings to try it. They hesitated.

David resumed eating, and Hugo copied his every move. Stefan finally helped himself to the tortilla and cottage cheese but paused to smell it before taking a nibble. Julia inspected the food Hugo gave her as if it was a laboratory specimen. When she noticed David's dirty look, she thrust it into her mouth in one big gulp. With their first bite out of the way, the siblings soon gobbled down their food. However, all three youths refused to touch the dried fish despite David's encouragement.

This food is even better than pizza! Hugo had to admit.

"What's this?" Stefan pointed to the oversized 'raisins.'

David was just about to pop an olive into his mouth. He let it roll out of his palm, landing on the ground. He gaped at Stefan. "They're dried figs."

They ate the rest of the meal in silence. David glowered, and Hugo guessed the shepherd didn't have good thoughts about them.

Hugo surveyed their surroundings more closely. The cliff with the cave was relatively high, making it impossible to climb down that way. It provided natural protection against anyone who might get the idea of stealing a sheep or two.

The sun was setting on the horizon, and it was getting noticeably colder. After the meal, David fetched a wooden harp from the cave and played. Hugo was instantly mesmerized by the beautiful sound and melodies coming from the instrument. He gazed, captivated, at the movement of David's fingers as he stroked the strings. After a while, the shepherd sang. "Praise to the Lord, O my soul, all that is within me praise his holy name. He is good and makes me whole. He forgives my sin and takes away my shame."

The songs went on for quite some time. Hugo felt a strange peace come over him. The words and music touched a part of his soul he didn't even know existed. *This guy should put his songs on YouTube. Or at least try to publish them. They're great.*

While sitting and listening to the music, Hugo looked up and held his breath in amazement at the number of stars. The sky was bursting with dots of light, small and large. He had never seen such a starry array before. He was also troubled by the lack of city lights in any direction. There was only darkness. *Where are we? And why are we stuck in the middle of nowhere?*

"Did you write those songs?" Julia asked when the music stopped. "They're beautiful."

David looked at them as if he had forgotten they were there. "Yes, I did."

Hugo was sure he detected a slight smile softening David's stoic face.

"You seem to have a very close relationship with God," Julia said, eyeing him curiously.

"He has brought me through a lot," David answered. "Just the other day, for example, a bear grabbed one of the sheep, but the Lord helped me chase it down and kill it."

The eyes of all three grew as big as the figs they had eaten. They were speechless.

"It doesn't happen often, thank the Lord." David stood up. "It's time to go to sleep. I hope I have enough sheepskins. Come into the cave with me."

They followed him inside. He held a small stone lamp that produced only a tiny ray of light.

"You will sleep in the cave," David said to Julia. He lifted the lamp to look at her face. "The rest of us will be outside."

The girl was horrified. "I don't want to stay here alone!" she protested. "Please, it's too dark and scary."

"You have no reason to be frightened. There's no other entrance, so no one else can get in, and we'll be right outside."

David must have meant to reassure her, but he had the opposite effect. Julia looked as if she was about to faint.

Stefan stepped forward and put his arm around his sister. "I can stay with her."

David was about to protest, then paused. "You're her brother, right?" Stefan nodded.

"Suit yourself."

David headed to a far corner and came back, holding more sheepskins. He handed two each to the siblings. "We have just enough," he said.

Julia and Stefan stared at the sheepskins, then at each other.

"What are they for?" Stefan asked.

David's head whipped around to face the boy. "You can sleep on the ground if you prefer."

Hugo suddenly understood they were to be his mattress. *You expect me to sleep on that thing? You're joking, right?* Hugo frowned. *Right?*

"What about blankets?" Stefan asked as David was leaving the cave.

"Use your cloak." There was a sharp tone to the shepherd's voice.

I better not ask about pillows.

Outside, Hugo reluctantly lay down on his so-called bed. The padding was minimal, and he could feel the rocks poking at him. Sleep was impossible in these conditions. To begin with, he was cold and uncomfortable, but even worse was the mental anguish. Questions and fears tormented him without ceasing. *Why are we here? Am I still dreaming? Have we somehow gotten stuck in a nightmare? Are we in danger? How can we get home?* Whenever he was about to nod off, thoughts of terror or distress attacked, jolting him back awake. He didn't know how long he tossed and turned before finally drifting off to sleep.

A few feet away, David was stretched out on his sheepskins by the entrance. He was wide awake and couldn't stop thinking about his strange guests and what to do with them. King Saul had given the order to be on the lookout for anyone suspicious, and he was certain these three kids were enemy spies. The Philistine army had attacked Israel, and they had surely sent out scouts to explore the land. His visitors didn't look like a threat—too young and clumsy—but their behavior would be the perfect disguise. What a slick move on their part. He didn't for one second believe their lost-wanderers-with-no-memory story. They were hiding something, and he had to be vigilant.

He had hoped to send them to his father the next day, but he realized he would have to wait for a servant to come since he couldn't leave the sheep unattended. He was stuck and not happy about it.

Lord, what should I do? I need your wisdom. He turned over on his sheepskins.

He couldn't leave them by themselves. He had to keep them from fulfilling their mission if they were Philistines, but in the unlikely event they were actually lost, they would be easy prey for the many robbers or wild animals roaming the land. He had no choice but to take them with him, although he suspected they would be nothing but trouble.

CHAPTER FOUR

THINGS AREN'T GOING AS PLANNED

"Wake up, sleepyhead!"

Hugo opened one eye at a time. He had no idea where he was. In a daze, he stared at David, holding the lamp. The events of the previous day slowly came back to him. It hadn't been a bad dream, after all. He really was in this strange place with this mysterious young shepherd and his smelly sheep.

He noticed how dark the sky was. "The sun isn't even up yet!" He rolled over to go back to sleep.

David poked the younger boy with his foot. "Where do you come from that you would sleep past dawn?" he asked and didn't stop prodding Hugo until he reluctantly sat up. David looked at the boy, disgusted.

Hugo tried to dispel the grogginess from his mind. *Where are you from that it's normal for a teen to get up before daybreak?*

David disappeared into the cave, and a pair of sleepy siblings emerged behind him after a while. Stefan had one eye still closed, and Julia couldn't stop yawning.

The menu for breakfast was the same as the previous evening. All three still refused to eat the fish, and David gave up trying to change their minds.

The shepherd briefly rechecked every sheep. He used a long walking stick that hooked at the end to bring them close to himself. It allowed him to hold the animals still for inspection. When finished, he packed rations in his leather pouch.

"Fortunately, I had a few extra water skins in the cave," he said as he handed them out. "We can fill them on the way."

Hugo and the siblings tied the water skins around their waists.

David hooked the wooden club to his belt and inspected the area one last time. He then grabbed his walking stick, and they headed out. The sun was barely peeking out behind the horizon.

"Where are we going?" asked Stefan.

"I'm taking the sheep out to graze."

"Do you always go to the same place?"

"Of course not! You really haven't been with sheep before, have you?"

Stefan looked away. "Not really," he whispered.

"So, you know nothing about sheep?"

The younger boy said nothing, but his face reddened.

David stopped to examine him. "Well, for your information, I have a favorite route I like to go. At this time of year, finding a good pasture is easy. Later in the summer, I take the sheep higher up into the hills."

The shepherd spun away from Stefan and stepped forward. He focused on keeping the sheep together as they walked while the other three quietly trudged behind. They slowly ascended along a canyon path, with rocky hills jetting up on both sides. The rising sun cast deep shadows, which made the terrain look surreal.

Hugo couldn't help but notice the sheep called Trouble behaved as David had described. The rebellious animal was causing the most problems, always wandering off in another direction. She even received the butt of David's club when she approached the edge of a steep incline. As she inched her way toward danger, the club swiftly flew through the air and hit her in the side. She bleated in shock and ran back towards the flock.

They arrived at a riverbed where a lazy brook was flowing. The kids watched with curiosity as David gathered large rocks to make a small dam, creating a pool of water. The sheep huddled around and drank deeply.

"What did you do that for?" Stefan asked.

David looked at the sky for a second and clenched his fists. "Sheep only drink when the water is still. They won't touch a flowing river or stream."

They filled their water skins and continued walking. They soon reached a plateau covered with coarse and uneven grass. It looked nothing like Pennsylvania's lush and deep-green lawns, but the sheep seemed happy enough as they eagerly set about grazing.

"We'll stay here," David announced, plopping down on one of the larger rocks. Hugo and the siblings sat down on the ground, only to jump back up at once. Their butts had big wet spots caused by the dew covering the grass.

David laughed. "Don't you know the grass is still moist at this hour?"

Julia, Stefan, and Hugo remained silent.

"You three are so strange," the shepherd remarked. "I mean, can you be completely ignorant about the basic things of life?" He locked his gaze on Hugo. "Or is it all an act?"

The boy swallowed. "As I told you, we lost our memories." He couldn't suppress the growing dread he was feeling.

"I know it's what you claim, but can you be so uneducated about even the simplest facts?"

Hugo suspected David wanted to provoke them into saying something to give away who they were. He was worried sick that the siblings would bite. He needed to talk to them alone, but the shepherd wasn't letting them out of his sight.

All at once, the sheep stopped their grazing and looked around uneasily. They quickly gathered closer together and became very agitated. A few bleated nervously.

All the muscles in David's body stiffened. "Don't move," he ordered. "Whatever happens, just stay calm."

Easier said than done. Hugo felt his body grow as cold as a popsicle. *Now what?*

"Here, hold my staff," David handed Stefan his walking stick. He leaped to his feet and dashed towards the sheep while scanning the rock-strewn hills surrounding the plateau where they had stopped. There were many places where someone, or something, could hide.

Hugo looked around but couldn't see anything to cause such alarm. Julia and Stefan inched towards him until they stood side by side. Hugo was sweating profusely, which caused his wool tunic to stick to his body. Suddenly, his face drained of all color.

Standing on a rock was a lion. Its majestic beauty would have amazed Hugo if he weren't so terrified of it. Compared to the caged lions Hugo had seen at the zoo, it was smaller and its mane was shorter, but it was more terrifying since there was no glass keeping him safe. The lion gave out such a fierce roar that Hugo's heart stopped beating for a second. The sound echoed off the rocky slopes.

As if in answer, David cried in a loud voice, "Praise be to the God of heaven, who protects his servants and gives them strength!" He sprinted to place himself between the sheep and the lion. With his sling, he launched a stone at the animal.

The lion crouched in time, and the projectile missed its mark. Enraged, it roared again and flung itself at David. The shepherd grabbed his club with both hands and lifted it high in the air while taking a step forward. When the lion was almost upon him, he rapidly brought it around and hit the attacking animal with a loud thud, catapulting it in the other direction. It flew five feet in the air and landed on its back, in total shock at what had just happened. It quickly bounced back on its feet and launched itself a second time at David. Miraculously, David repeated his counterattack and launched the lion off course again.

This time, when the lion recovered from its unintended flight, it paused as if thinking the matter over. Abruptly, it turned around and disappeared behind a boulder with one bound.

David hurried towards the sheep. They were pressed up against each other in an almost perfect circle. He spoke softly to them to calm them down, petting each one in turn, and they gradually relaxed. One by one, they went back to grazing.

Julia, Hugo, and Stefan watched him in awe. No one said a word. When the young shepherd was sure the sheep were relaxed, he came back to where his three guests were huddling together.

"It won't come back," he said. "It must have realized it wasn't worth it. There is easier prey to catch." He laughed.

"Awesome!" Stefan said. His eyes glistened. "You were incredible."

"The Lord helped me. Besides, being with the sheep so much, I have a lot of time to train how to fight." David patted his club before attaching it to his belt. "My sweet rod, we've been through a lot together." He took his staff back from Stefan.

"How could you be so sure God would help?" asked Julia. "You didn't even hesitate."

"Why wouldn't he?" David asked. "The Lord promised he would." He looked up at the sky. "He's never failed me in the past. I always ask for his strength, and he always delivers."

"It can't be so simple," she said. "If a lion attacked me and I prayed for help, I doubt I could fight it off."

"I see your point." He smiled. "Just as we train our muscles to get stronger, we must exercise our faith for it to grow. I've been training both for years, and you haven't. However, you can always start."

Hugo listened to the conversation with fascination. *How is such confidence even possible?*

"Do lions attack often?" Stefan asked.

"Fortunately not, but it's not the first one I've faced."

"I can't believe you were willing to die for your sheep!"

"I wouldn't be a good shepherd if I weren't. It's my job to protect them."

"But they're only going to get killed anyway. You said so yourself. Why risk your life for nothing?"

David's eyes burned with such fury that Stefan's cheeks turned crimson red, and his shoulders drooped. He took a step back.

"First of all, until their final day, I want them to have a happy life. Secondly, they don't deserve to be torn to pieces and eaten alive. And thirdly, my family's income would suffer." David was so outraged he was shaking. "So if this lion returns, I should let it attack and eat you. After all, you'll die someday too. Right?" He glared at Stefan.

The boy lowered his head. "No," he mumbled.

"My sheep deserve my protection, and my family expects me to take good care of them. My reputation as a shepherd is at stake." He looked over at the flock. "Besides, I can't let them down. They're helpless and depend on me. Whenever anything bad happens to one of them, I feel rotten. I can't let that happen." He angrily kicked a rock. It went flying and almost hit one of the animals.

"You really love your sheep, don't you?" asked Julia.

The shepherd nodded. "The cry of a sheep being ripped apart has haunted my nights." His eyes had a distant faraway look, and Hugo was sure they moistened slightly. David spun around and hurried back to tend to the flock.

Hugo remained silent, deeply touched by his words.

"I love Domino so much, but I wouldn't fight a lion to save him," Julia whispered.

Hugo looked at her and nodded. "Same with my dog, Gibson."

The three sat down, this time on rocks. Hugo tried to relax, taking a deep breath, but too much adrenaline flowed through his veins. He worried about David. If he could dispose of a lion so easily, Hugo didn't want to imagine what the shepherd could do to them.

David came back to sit nearby.

"Don't you get bored being out with the sheep all the time?" asked Stefan.

"I told you to stop pestering him with so many questions." Julia scowled at her brother, who stuck out his tongue at her.

David watched the two siblings, and a hint of a smile appeared on his face.

"I'm never bored. There's always too much to do. For example, the minor task of fighting a lion."

"Don't you have any free time? What do you like doing?" Stefan asked. He looked at Julia in defiance.

"What's free time?" David looked confused at even the concept of such a thing.

"Don't you have time to relax?"

"Relax?" He laughed. "I play my harp in the evenings when the flock is safe in the sheepfold, and I compose songs and poems. You heard some of them yesterday. They're mostly prayers to God. And I'm always training my fighting skills."

Both Hugo and Stefan perked up. "How?" Stefan asked.

"I have seven older brothers. There's been no lack of battles in our house." David's eyes darkened to reflect a deep sadness.

"I don't have any brothers," Hugo said, "or sisters either. I always wished I did. It's lonely growing up alone."

"I sometimes wished I didn't." David turned thoughtful. He then frowned and looked over at Hugo. "So, you haven't lost your memory after all." His eyes narrowed.

Hugo flushed, furious at himself for possibly putting them in danger. "Some things I remember, but not much." He ran out of anything else to say.

"What weapons do you fight with?" Stefan asked. For once, Hugo was grateful for the boy's insatiable curiosity.

"My hands, my sling, and my rod. Sometimes with a knife, and in the king's service, I've learned to use a sword."

"A sword!" The younger boy's eyes and mouth opened wide.

Hugo couldn't believe it. *What kind of a backward place is this?*

David went to round up a few sheep that had wandered too far away while Hugo stood up to stretch his legs. The rest of the day went by without further incident until the sun started its descent in the sky.

"It's time to make our way back to the sheepfold," David announced. He walked towards the sheep and yelled the same strange call he had used the previous day. As before, the animals came running towards him. He inspected and counted each one. When assured all were present, he led them down the same trail they had taken on the way up.

They walked in silence. Stefan traipsed alongside the flock, observing the landscape, when he pointed to something nearby. "What's that?"

David leaned over to see what he was talking about, then grimaced in irritation. "It's what's left of a wild goat. Can't you tell?"

"No," Stefan muttered.

"These hills are full of predators. Skeletons are everywhere." David scanned the horizon while the younger boy shuddered.

They resumed their descent. Suddenly, the shepherd stopped in mid-stride and cocked his ear. Hugo noticed a strange sound that hadn't been there before. Alarmed, they continued downward as the noise grew louder until they finally came to its source. The ambling stream they had crossed on the way up was now a full-blown river. It wasn't deep, but the current was strong. The sheep bleated nervously.

"Where did *that* come from?" Stefan asked.

"Rain and melting snow upstream always cause this river to swell in the spring. And, of course, it would have to be today!" David raised his arms in frustration and mouthed, "Why?" He headed towards the bank. "Stay here with the sheep, I'll go check it out."

He walked about thirty feet in each direction, evaluating the river. After determining the best place to cross, he slowly entered the water and shivered. The river reached no higher than his thighs. He felt his way about halfway across and then turned around and came back to them.

"We're going to cross over there." He pointed to where he had entered. "You'll each have to carry a lamb, and I'll take the last two. The older sheep will be okay."

Julia recoiled at the shepherd's words. She looked at Hugo and whispered, "I'm afraid of water."

"You'll be all right," he said to encourage her, but his words fell flat. He could see she was terrified.

Stefan, on the other hand, looked excited. Some more adventure!

David handed a lamb to each one. Hugo almost let go of his animal at once. The little fellow squirmed in his arms, trying with all its might to break free. To make matters worse, its mother was poking him with her nose, showing her displeasure.

"No matter what you do, don't let go until you're on the other side. I'll go in first, you come behind me, and the sheep will follow."

He picked up the last two lambs, one under each arm. Hugo noticed he was talking to himself and wondered if he were praying. David called out to the sheep and slowly entered the river.

The shock of the freezing water almost made Hugo let go of his lamb, but he recovered in time. The deeper he went, the more difficulty he had keeping his balance. The river was so cold he couldn't keep his teeth from chattering. He had to fight against the current. The little animal in his arms was whining. Stefan and Julia waded through the water next to him. He could see they were struggling just as much as he was.

Curious about the sheep, Hugo turned to see what they were doing. Some had boldly entered the river at once, while others hesitated. The last one bleated and struck the ground with her hoofs as if in protest, but when she noticed she was alone on the bank, she timidly followed the others into the water. Despite the current, all were able to make slow forward progress. Only their heads stuck out of the water, and from a distance, they looked like a paddling of ducks.

David reached the other side and gently placed the lambs on the ground. They frolicked about with joy. Julia smiled at their sight, which distracted her for a second. She suddenly lost her balance and fell backward into the water, splashing Stefan and Hugo. As a natural reflex to regain her balance, she straightened out her arms, letting go of the lamb. The current got a hold of the tiny animal, and before anyone could react, the river swept it downstream. Its pitiful frightened cry echoed off the surface of the water until it disappeared.

David acted quickly. "Follow me," he shouted at Hugo, who had reached the riverbank. He then looked at Stefan and Julia. "Take care of the sheep until we return, and don't go anywhere." He bolted in the direction of the lost lamb.

Hugo dashed after him but struggled to keep up with David, and he promptly tripped and fell. Anxiety took over his thoughts. What help could he be to David? He was sure to mess things up and do more harm than good.

As they ran, they again caught sight of the lamb. The current was picking up speed the further down they went. The river took a sharp turn to the right, and the frightened animal disappeared.

When they got around the bend, they saw the stream had turned into a short series of rapids, which leveled off into a flat section where the current slowed considerably. There was no lamb anywhere. David paused for a moment to assess the situation, his eyes scanning the water. Suddenly, a tiny head emerged from the water. It was pinned up against a rock formation in the middle of the river. They could tell it was still alive by its desperate attempts to stay afloat.

"There!" David pointed toward the lamb. They made their way down toward the animal as quickly as possible. The steep riverbank was slippery and tricky to walk on. Even David stumbled, which gave Hugo some guilty pleasure.

They finally reached the bottom and hurried to where the lamb struggled to stay above water. David smiled.

"The river is much calmer here," he said. "This won't take long." He handed his staff to Hugo and entered the river. He made his way through waist-high water towards the lamb, which bleated when it saw him. The shepherd quickly reached the little animal and took it in his arms as gently as possible. Before heading back, he paused to allow the lamb to relax.

Hugo was calmly watching the rescue operation until something caught his eye. He took a step closer to get a better look. He gasped, and panic filled his thoughts when he realized what he was seeing. A snake was swimming straight towards David, who had his back to it.

Hugo wanted to yell a warning, but his mouth refused to cooperate. The more he tried, the more panic took over as he felt his throat constrict to the point where he could barely breathe, just like on *the day*. Hugo felt frozen in place and time. All he could do was watch in horror as the reptile slithered toward the shepherd and the lamb.

When the snake was no more than a few inches away, David finally turned around and saw it. He let go of the lamb and grabbed the snake just behind its head. With all his might, he threw it towards land. The reptile flew a good twenty feet in the air and landed on the far side of the river. David then turned his attention toward the little sheep, which had started to sink. He plucked it out of the water, held it close, and headed to shore. When he climbed onto the bank, he sat down and let go of the lamb. It took a few unsteady steps and then collapsed right next to David, shaking.

"I don't mean to complain, but you could have warned me about the snake," David said. He made eye contact with Hugo as if trying to decipher his thoughts.

Hugo felt his cheeks flush and lowered his gaze to the ground. Something in David's stare bothered him. *Does he think I wanted him dead?* He was too embarrassed to even look at the shepherd. He had failed—as he knew he would. *I'm such a loser.* He burned with shame.

"I'm sorry," Hugo finally said in a whisper. He could still feel David's piercing glare but didn't dare lift his head. "I panicked. I wanted to yell, but no words would come out of my mouth, no matter how hard I tried. I felt like someone was choking me." He hoped the shepherd believed him.

There was a long pause. "We better get back to the others. Getting the lamb has taken much longer than I thought. I hope your friends haven't let any of my sheep wander off." David glanced at the small animal lying by his side and gently petted its head. He then picked it up and put it over his shoulders, two legs on each side of his neck.

They made their way back up the slope. Climbing was much smoother than going down, and they quickly reached the turn in the river. When they went around the bend, they immediately realized something was wrong. It was much too quiet. They should have heard bleating and talking, but only silence met them. David dashed forward, leaving Hugo behind, who sprinted to catch up, fear pumping strength into his arms and legs. When they reached the place where they had crossed the river, no one was there.

CHAPTER FIVE

KIDNAPPED

David quickly dropped the lamb to the ground. He hurled his staff into the dirt and screamed at the top of his lungs. Hugo looked around, sweat pouring down his forehead into his eyes. His hands trembled. A few sheep and all the lambs appeared. They ran towards their shepherd and greeted him with joy. David patted their heads absentmindedly while analyzing the area. Several more sheep came running. One of them was the mother of the lamb they had rescued, and the shepherd smiled despite himself at their happy reunion.

"What happened?" Hugo finally dared to ask.

"They've been captured by raiders, probably Philistines."

"What do you mean?"

"Those brutes will add my sheep to their flocks and sell your friends as slaves."

"No!" Hugo felt as if he was going to suffocate. This mysterious adventure was becoming more and more like a horror movie. Its dangers were real, and Hugo didn't know how to deal with the terror taking over his thoughts.

"I'm going after them. You'll stay here and watch the sheep. Here's my staff to help you."

Hugo didn't argue. David was right to not want to take him along. He would only cause trouble. He was a coward, after all. He reluctantly took the staff.

"Why didn't they take all the sheep?" Hugo asked. Having to guard them made him uneasy, as he was sure to botch such a simple task as well.

"They probably thought too many animals would slow them down, especially the lambs." He then smirked. "They took my dear Trouble with them. She'll delay them all right." He turned toward Hugo. "Don't get yourself kidnapped. Trust in the Lord and be of good courage." David took off running and disappeared behind the crest of a hill.

Hugo sat down on a rock and looked around at what was left of the flock. A rage overcame him, and he grabbed a pebble and threw it into the river with all his might. He hated this place and longed to be back home, in his world, where he knew how to operate. Here, even the most basic daily task was a mystery.

A theory about where they were had started to take shape in his mind, and it terrified him. His friends were in real danger, and he couldn't do a thing to help them. His thoughts turned to what they might be going through, and his anger morphed into anxiety and fear. For the first time, he realized how much he loved them. They were more than his friends. They were the brother and sister he had never had.

Several of the sheep wandered too far away. *Oh no, you don't!* He jumped to his feet and used David's staff to herd the meandering animals back toward the remaining flock. He was a bit too abrupt in his movements and frightened the others, who dispersed in all directions.

Please don't do this to me. Hugo attempted to repeat David's call to gather the sheep, but they completely ignored him. He picked up a few pebbles and tried throwing them in the path of the roaming animals, but it only made things worse. He hit a sheep in the head, causing it to scurry even faster.

Defeated, he screamed at the top of his lungs, releasing all his frustrations. He then sat down and placed his head in his hands, taking deep breaths to calm himself. The lamb rescued from the river approached him and nudged him with its nose. Hugo took it in his arms and hugged it, trying to find comfort in its soft wool. Its mother stood nearby as if approving.

He held on to the lamb for a long time, allowing his emotions to subside. He then noticed all the sheep had come back and were standing around him. At least, he hoped it was all of them. Otherwise, David would be livid, and Hugo didn't want to be the object of the young shepherd's wrath.

Meanwhile, David was making good progress in tracking the raiders. They had left an easy trail to follow. At the pace they were going, he would quickly catch up. The problem was what to do when he reached them. The sun was setting on the horizon, and he figured they wouldn't get to their land before sundown, forcing them to camp for the night. He would have to strike then.

He thought about the events of the last twenty-four hours. Ever since his strange guests had appeared out of the blue, he'd had nothing but problems. At least he was now sure they weren't Philistine spies. Otherwise, the raiders would have left them alone. Despite all his skepticism towards them, he dreaded to think what would happen once they crossed the border. He pressed on.

The sun went down, but the moon shone so brightly it cast a pale light everywhere. In the distance, he could see the glow of a campfire, and he smiled. He quietly approached the place where the raiders had settled for the night with their loot.

In the moonlight, he counted six Philistine soldiers. Two were guarding the perimeter, two were making a temporary sheepfold out of tangled thorn bushes, one was watching Stefan and Julia, and the last one was tending to the fire.

David crawled closer, not making a sound. He observed the siblings, tied up by their hands and feet, sitting on the ground. Julia looked around, wide-eyed and shaking. Stefan leaned toward his sister.

"Shut up!" The man guarding them kicked the boy in the abdomen. Stefan yelped and doubled over in agony, but the raider continued to hit him. Julia sat still, too frightened to move.

When David saw the raider strike the boy, compassion filled his heart. In an instant, all the irritation, doubt, and suspicion he felt toward them melted away. For the first time, he saw them as the lost and confused wanderers they claimed to be. *Lord, may you give your servant success.*

He waited until most activities had quieted down for the night. Two perimeter guards were keeping watch. Another man looked after the sheep while the other three were sleeping. Julia and Stefan were sitting halfway between the animals and the slumbering men. They were scanning their surroundings as if looking for something. *Could they be waiting for me?* David wondered and couldn't stop himself from smiling.

The time to act had finally come. David crept up quietly on the two perimeter guards, who were standing about twenty feet apart. He sent two stones flying through the air with his sling, one right after the other, hitting both sentries and knocking them out cold. David didn't even stop to check if they were dead or alive, confident that they wouldn't bother him any time soon. He paused to hear if any of the other raiders had become alarmed. Everything was quiet.

The Philistine watching over the sheep was looking in the other direction. *You fool*, David smirked. The raider must have been deep in thought not to hear the thump of the two falling guards. David silently slid up behind him, and before the man knew what was happening, David launched another stone and hit him in the back of the head. He slumped to the ground in a loud crash, causing some sheep to become agitated and bleat.

The sleeping men woke up and jumped to their feet, grabbing their weapons. The closest one wasn't fast enough, and he quickly fell to the ground. A stone had hit him square in the face. There were two raiders left.

When Julia and Stefan noticed David, they crawled toward the improvised sheepfold. They could only slide forward a few inches at a time because of the cords binding their hands and feet. When they reached the crude fence, they pulled the thorn bushes apart to let the sheep out. The sharp briers scratched and hurt, but they kept going.

One of the raiders noticed what they were doing. Infuriated, he sprang in their direction, sword drawn, ready to strike. David saw him, but he was too far away to help, and the other Philistine was coming straight toward him. A deep guttural cry to God for help rose within him, and he felt something he didn't usually feel—panic. In desperation, he smashed the attacking raider in the head with his rod. The Philistine was still falling when David turned around to see what was happening to the siblings and witnessed an incredible scene.

When the raider reached Stefan and Julia, he shouted a victory cry and, with both hands, lifted his sword high in the air. At that moment, Trouble charged through the opening the siblings had made in the thorn bushes. She went straight for the attacker. He was about to slice the siblings to pieces when she whacked him at full speed, striking him right between the legs. He doubled over in pain and let out a soft moan as he collapsed to the ground, dropping his weapon.

David cheered and then burst out laughing. He rushed towards the fallen raider and stood over him for a few seconds before picking up his sword to cut the ropes which bound the siblings. He was still laughing when he tied up the Philistine by his wrists and ankles. The shepherd almost felt sorry for the man, who was clearly still in pain.

"By the time he's recovered and the others wake up, we'll be long gone."

When David glanced at his sheep, especially Trouble, he felt like kicking the man in the same painful place again. The animal was covered in wounds, some of which were still bleeding. "Whatever happened to you?" He gently patted her head. Treating her injuries would have to wait. They had to get going as quickly as possible.

David counted his sheep, and remembering which ones were with Hugo, he was pleased to note none were missing. He recovered their stolen water skins and took the raiders' food pouches, keeping only the olives and fig cakes.

After looking around one last time, they took off, and the sheep followed without causing any problems, even Trouble.

"I knew you would come!" Stefan gazed at David with awe and admiration. "You're a real Superman."

David had no idea what Stefan was talking about, but he smiled at the gratitude he could hear in the boy's voice.

"I don't know how to thank you!" Julia beamed. "Those men were horrible. I hate to think what would have happened if you hadn't come!" She shivered.

"Oh, they would have sold you as slaves," David said without emotion. "I only came to save my sheep. You just happened to benefit." He winked at them and laughed, then turned serious. "Tell me what happened."

"After you left, the sheep tried to follow you. We were gathering them back together when those men appeared out of nowhere and surrounded us." Julia blanched at the memory. "They tied our arms behind us and made us walk—along with most of the flock." She flinched. "They were horrible!"

David noticed bruises on their faces and guessed similar marks covered the rest of their bodies.

"They hit you, didn't they?" He didn't know which emotion he felt the most—sadness or anger.

The siblings nodded. Julia bit her lip. "Whenever we couldn't keep pace, they beat us with a stick. They kicked us until we got back up if we stumbled and fell."

"But you should have seen the sheep you call Trouble!" Stefan interjected. "She was trouble for them all right." He snickered. "That's why they beat her so much, and with the same stick they used to hit us."

David glared, anger rising within him. He felt like striking something, preferably a Philistine.

"But she got back at them." Stefan's eyes shone brightly. "We had stopped for a moment, and the man with the stick turned his back to her. She lowered her head and ran forward with all her might. She hit him smack in the rear end and sent him flying." He burst out laughing.

David turned to look at Trouble. "Good girl!" He was proud of her.

As they walked, they drank from the water skins and ate what they kept from the captured provisions, making sure to save some for Hugo. Refreshed with new energy, they picked up the pace.

"You were incredible. I mean, you defeated all those men," Stefan exclaimed.

"The Lord is the one who gave me strength. I couldn't have done it without him," David said. "And besides, he sent Trouble at just the right time."

"If God is so strong, why didn't he stop those men from kidnapping us in the first place?" Julia asked. "Wouldn't his task have been so much simpler?" She turned to face David, as if daring him to come up with an answer.

"You've asked an excellent question." The young shepherd gave her a weak smile. He paused as he pondered how to answer. "I guess it's because the Lord has given people the freedom to choose between good and evil."

Julia frowned. "But why?"

"I've wondered the same myself," David admitted. "I doubt we can fully understand why, but I suspect it all comes down to love."

"What do you mean? You're not even making sense."

The shepherd became thoughtful. "When you love someone, you want them to love you back, but it's not something you can force. Do you agree?"

Julia nodded.

"So, it's no different with God." David looked at her and could tell she struggled to grasp his meaning. "The Lord cares for us and wants our affection in return, but he gives us a choice to love or reject him, which means that people can do bad things if they wish. Sadly, we've become masters at doing evil."

"God has a strange way of showing his love," Julia said.

"You might be complaining even more if you weren't free to choose." David stopped walking and lifted his eyes to the sky. "Look, there's a lot I don't understand, but this one thing I know—I can trust the Lord completely." His voice rang out with conviction.

"Why?"

"Because he's good and has always helped me when I needed him."

Julia looked at David with both amazement and suspicion but remained quiet. They continued without further conversation. David was exhausted. The adrenaline was wearing off, and he felt the effects of the constant stress of having three unusual guests. He couldn't wait to get back to the sheepfold.

Back by the river, Hugo was miserable, cold, and uncomfortable. He thought of his room at home with his bed, computer, and faithful Gibson. Man, did he miss them! He wished he could whip out his phone and call David for the latest news. He agonized over the fate of his friends.

He was also fed up with the sheep, having had to continually corral them until they got so tired they finally settled down. The life of a shepherd was not for him.

He sat on the ground, slumped forward with his chin resting in his hands. He relived in his mind the events leading up to being in this strange place—the nightmares, meeting Julia and Stefan, the secret room—and wondered what it all meant. He had the feeling they were all connected somehow.

He thought about David's last words to him and gasped when he realized they were the exact quote he had read on the wall of the secret room, "Be of good courage." But instead of encouraging him, they mockingly highlighted his cowardice compared to David's bravery. He fell into despair and self-loathing.

A surprising thought broke through his anguish. *You can discover David's secret and be like him.* Hugo laughed at such a bold declaration, but a growing excitement countered his mockery. Was it even possible for him to change? Hugo sat up straight as a glimmer of hope appeared on the horizon of his soul.

A few sheep bleated and paced the area. Before long, all the animals were agitated. Hugo became distressed, and all his anxiety returned. Being like David wasn't going to be easy. He thought he heard a noise. Could it be footsteps?

Before he had the time to process it all, some fluffy, white forms appeared from over the hill, and then, three human silhouettes became visible in the distance. He recognized them instantly.

"Julia! Stefan!" he squealed, leaping to his feet. "David, you did it!" He sprinted towards them, laughing. He gave the siblings a bone-crushing hug, and they hugged him back just as tightly. He let go of them and approached the shepherd. Not knowing how to behave, he awkwardly grabbed his arm and slapped him on the shoulder. David grinned at him.

"Thanks." Hugo couldn't think of anything else to say.

"Here's some food. You must be starving." David handed him a pouch, and Hugo's stomach growled as if in answer, reminding him he was famished.

He ate ravenously as Julia and Stefan recounted their harrowing experience. While they were so occupied, David called the sheep and inspected each one as best he could in the moonlight. When he finished, he frowned and rubbed his chin with his fingers. Hugo noticed the shepherd's puzzled look and felt a knot in his stomach. It could only mean one thing. He had difficulty focusing on what the siblings said as David counted the flock a second time.

Julia was recounting Trouble's attack on the raider when David rushed over to them, visibly distressed. She stopped speaking when she saw him. David ran right up to Hugo and grabbed him by his cloak. He dragged Hugo up to eye level, almost lifting him clear off the ground. He brought the boy's face to within an inch of his own. His cheeks were red with fury.

"One of my sheep is missing," he yelled, staring deep into Hugo's eyes. "What have you done?"

CHAPTER SIX

AN UNEXPECTED TURN OF EVENTS

Hugo's mind went blank. David let go of him and stomped away, trembling. Hugo stood motionless, convinced any movement would cause more of David's wrath to come his way. Devastated, he fought hard to keep himself from trembling.

David marched back and forth, trying to rein in his emotions. "Let's get back to the sheepfold," he barked. "Then I'll go looking for her."

No one said a word.

"Move!"

They promptly took off. Even the sheep knew better than to disobey their master, and they followed behind obediently.

Thanks to the brisk pace David set, they quickly reached the sheepfold. Everyone, human and animal, was relieved to enter its welcoming confines.

David refused to look at Hugo. "One of you should stay awake and sit in the doorway while the others sleep. Don't let the sheep go anywhere, you hear me?" They nodded. "In fact, don't do anything at all until I get back. You might ruin something."

David turned and bolted through the entryway. They watched him go in silence until he disappeared into the night.

Hugo was the first to speak. "I'm so sorry. I did everything I could to keep those dumb sheep together. How could I know one of them was missing? They all look the same." His head dropped. "I always end up messing everything up."

Julia and Stefan came over to hug him. He was grateful for their gesture but didn't feel the comfort he desired.

"David's going to hate me from now on. What's going to happen to us?" Hugo's voice shook.

"I think he'll forgive you," Julia said, her eyes shining with surprising confidence.

"How can you be so certain? I thought he was going to kill me." Hugo cringed at the memory of David's outburst.

"Because he has a good heart."

He looked at her, surprised. "I'm not so sure, but I hope he finds the stupid sheep. He'll be more forgiving then."

The siblings nodded.

"I'll sit in the gateway first," Hugo said, "but before you go to sleep, we need to talk about something else." Now was finally his chance to speak openly with them.

Julia and Stefan went to retrieve the sheepskins, and all three sat down by the entrance to the pen. The softness and warmth of the pelts were absolute paradise, and even the smell was no longer a problem.

"So, where do you think we are?" Hugo asked. Before anyone could answer, he continued, "I think we were drugged, kidnapped, and then brought here by psychopaths to take part in a sick reality show to see if kids from the twenty-first century could survive in the ancient world."

"I don't think a show like this would be allowed to exist," Julia said, eyeballing him dubiously.

"Why not?" Hugo asked. "They say the dark web is full of all sorts of crazy things."

"Your theory makes sense," Stefan exclaimed. "We're like in a giant escape room."

"You two are way off base," Julia said, rolling her eyes. The boys drew back in surprise.

"By all means, clue us in." Hugo gestured sarcastically.

"Do you remember what happened before we showed up here?"

"How could we not? We were in the strange secret room and looking at the old Bible. So?"

"Right. We were staring at the pages, which had beautiful illustrations. Remember the last picture of a shepherd boy with his sheep?" She waited for them to nod. "Then, everything started spinning." She paused as if afraid to say what came next. "I think David is that shepherd boy."

They stared at her incredulously until the words sunk in. Hugo's mouth dropped open.

"You mean to say we somehow entered the Bible story?" He could barely get the words out. He burst out laughing at the absurdity of her theory. Stefan joined him.

"I knew you would react this way." Julia scowled at them. "I can't explain it, but it's the only thing that makes sense. More than your crazy idea, anyway." She slapped Hugo on the shoulder. "Think about it for a second. Since we're thousands of years in the past—or however long ago we are—it's no wonder the people here don't know anything about our world, and—"

"This is the silliest theory I've ever heard," Hugo said.

"It's better than thinking we're on some sick reality show," she scoffed.

"At least my theory has us somewhere during our lifetime," Hugo said.

"I don't think they could make a set big enough to include all the distance we've traveled. And where are they hiding the cameras?" She looked at Hugo smugly. "Why all this God talk from David?" she continued. "You would think they would avoid it." The boys remained silent.

"Assuming we are in a Bible story," Hugo remarked, not without a tinge of sarcasm, "how in the world did we get here? And more importantly, how can we return home?"

"I don't know," she sighed.

"And how come we speak the language?"

Julia remained silent.

"If we have gone back to the past to relive some story in the Bible," he said, "then we better not say a word about our world. Nothing." He glanced at Stefan.

"Don't tell me you believe her!" The younger boy sat up straight and crossed his arms.

"I don't know what to believe," Hugo said, "I'm just saying we have to be very careful about what we say, regardless of whether we are thousands of years in the past, on a reality show, or somewhere else. If we say the wrong thing, we may get in serious trouble. Understood?"

The siblings nodded.

"And we all agree to keep telling David we've lost our memory. Okay?"

"Yes, sir." They gave a mock salute.

When the weight of Julia's words hit Hugo with full force, his hands started trembling, and he quickly folded them under his armpits to keep them from shaking. The idea of being on a deadly show had been scary enough, but Julia's theory horrified him. "I had wanted us to try to escape, but if you're correct, there's nowhere to run." His shoulders slumped.

"We'll have to ask discreet questions to see if I'm right," Julia said. She looked at her brother and Hugo, who thought he saw a tear roll down her cheek. "No matter the truth, I only want to go home." Her voice quivered.

The boys dropped their heads. Hugo squashed his growing homesickness before it had the chance to overwhelm him. Now was not the time for such longing.

"It's the middle of the night. We should get some sleep," Hugo said.

Julia stood up and stretched. "Man, I could sure use a shower right now."

"Yeah. I've been meaning to tell you but didn't know how. You really stink," Hugo said, barely suppressing a smile.

"How dare you!" Julia stomped her foot and clenched her fists while the boys burst out laughing. She pointed at her brother. "Don't even say a word."

Stefan ran his fingers over his mouth as if zipping it closed, but his body shook from laughter.

"Go back to the cave and sleep," Hugo said when he calmed down, "I'll keep watch here. After an hour, I'll wake one of you up to take my place."

"How will you know the time? You don't have a phone." Stefan gave him a mischievous grin.

"Don't be such a smart aleck." Hugo kicked him playfully.

"I'm just learning from you." The younger boy stood up and gladly walked to the cave, with his sister trailing behind.

Hugo placed a sheepskin in the entrance to the sheepfold and sat down. It didn't take long for his eyes to close and his head to bobble, but he shook himself awake each time until his eyelids became so heavy he could no longer pry them open. He was soon sound asleep.

Meanwhile, David reached the place where they had crossed the river. He realized he should have expected the sheep's disappearance. She was the one who never wanted to leave his side, so it's no wonder she went looking for him. He reluctantly admitted it wasn't Hugo's fault after all.

He'd rescued her from a fox's mouth when she was a tiny lamb, and she'd been utterly devoted to him ever since. He unofficially called her "Pushy" because she always pushed the other animals out of her way to get close to him.

Chances were slim that she was still alive. There were so many dangers for a sheep alone in the wilderness. Not only could she easily hurt herself by her clumsiness and foolishness, but many predators roamed the land, waiting to pounce.

He stared at the river as if trying to gain inspiration from its rushing waters, but instead, darkness clouded his soul. Pushy's disappearance was the last straw, causing his exasperation to burst within him like an old brittle waterskin filled with too much water. All his resentment towards his three guests returned.

"Why do I have to take care of those dimwits?" He yelled at the sky. "Did you send them to me? Is this a test of leadership? Well, thanks! If you wanted to torment me, you've succeeded. And now, because of them, Pushy is in danger. How could you have let her wander off? What has she ever done to deserve this?"

The only answer he got in return was silence.

David stood and continued by retracing the route he had followed to track the Philistine raiders. The longer he walked, the more his anger made it difficult to take a step. He couldn't focus on the basic task of putting one foot in front of the other.

Unable to go further, he collapsed to the ground. Looking around at the moonlit landscape, he knew finding the sheep would take a miracle. He sat motionless, unsure of what to do next. Should he go back?

The thought hit him like a clay jar full of oil. *You have compassion for your missing sheep but refuse to show mercy to the three lost wanderers. Be kindhearted toward people, too—not just animals.*

The criticism stung. A picture formed in David's mind where he saw a fortress with thick walls and a heavy wooden door bolted shut.

This is your heart.

David instantly understood. He had let the abuse and mistreatment of his past make him cold and callous, pushing others away. As a result, he couldn't show the compassion God wanted.

"Lord, I need your help. I'm so sorry." He looked up and repeated the words, not once, but twice, and louder each time.

He was about to stand up and turn around to leave when he noticed a small ravine about twenty feet away. As he stared at it absentmindedly, he was filled with a strong urge to enter it, as if an internal voice was saying to him, *Go in there.* At first, he ignored it, but then he recognized who was speaking.

Thank you, Lord. He jumped to his feet and dashed toward the ravine. It started wide and shallow, but soon its walls became steep and high, and the passageway narrowed to fit only one person.

After cautiously making his way through the ravine for a few minutes, he began to have doubts. Was this the right place? Yet the voice in his heart had been so strong.

While contemplating whether or not to turn around, he heard a noise. He paused to listen and quickly realized it was the bleating of a sheep. He surged forward and promptly tripped over some unseen object. More carefully this time, he continued straight ahead in the direction of the sound.

The ravine turned sharply to the right, and bright moonlight greeted him as he went around the bend. The high walls widened considerably, and Pushy stood before him. She had her back to him and was bleating excitedly, craning her neck towards him as much as possible. He rushed forward. *Thank you, Lord!*

He quickly noticed why she wasn't moving. Her front legs were tangled in a root. He walked around her to free the captive limbs and saw he was standing near the edge of a cliff. He turned to observe the view before him. He was high up on the side of a hill.

Thank you, Lord, for this root that kept Pushy from plunging to certain death.

David carefully picked her up and put her on his shoulders. He turned and slowly made his way back through the ravine, then picked up the pace once out in the open. He carried Pushy the whole way, willing himself to get to the sheepfold as quickly as possible. His adrenaline and joy at finding her gave him strength despite his exhaustion.

When he got to the sheepfold, he stopped in front of Hugo asleep across the entryway. *I see how well you're guarding the place.* He stared at the snoozing boy for a few seconds, but compassion filled his soul instead of anger. *I must have scared the poor guy to death.* David regretted his outburst. He carefully stepped over the boy, making sure not to wake him, and gently put the sheep down on the ground. How grateful he was, and how tired! He noticed the sheepskins Hugo had left for him, and he was fast asleep the moment his head hit the ground.

A few hours later, the sun shone brightly as the siblings shuffled about the sheepfold while Hugo stood in the entrance, observing the sleeping shepherd. He hoped the sheep lying virtually on top of David was the lost one. He wanted to run away, but there was nowhere to go. Besides, what about his newfound resolve to be like David? No, he had to face whatever happened head-on.

David stirred. He opened his eyes and looked confused at the sheep sleeping on him. His face lit up in a smile as he nudged the animal and sat up.

"You found her, didn't you?" Julia said.

Hugo stiffened. David glanced over at him, and their eyes met. Hugo quickly looked away.

"Hugo! Can you come here for a moment?"

How could he disobey? He reluctantly walked towards the shepherd while studying the ground. He braced himself for a chewing-out, or worse. Was this how it felt to walk down death row?

David stood up to face him. "Hugo, I'm sorry." He reached out to put his hand on the boy's shoulder. "I'm sure you did all you could to keep the sheep together. I should have never yelled at you like that."

Hugo was speechless. He stood in a daze, not quite grasping what was happening.

"Can you forgive me?" David asked.

It took all of Hugo's strength to look up and make eye contact, and he saw regret and sadness on the shepherd's face. A few moments passed while the boy processed David's words and realized he was sincere. He then beamed with joy and amazement. "Of course, I forgive you!" he exclaimed, eyes shining bright. "But I'm the one who failed. You should be the one forgiving me."

"I have."

Warmth filled Hugo's body.

David slapped him on the back. "So, now that's settled, let's change the subject. I'm starving." He turned to fetch the food pouches from the cave.

While eating the same thing as the day before, the three couldn't resist peppering David with questions. They wanted to know how he had managed to find the lost sheep, and he could barely get a bite in as he told them what happened.

When he finished eating, David stood up. "I have to take care of my flock. It's already so late." He walked towards the sheep, concluding the conversation.

He meticulously examined the condition of each animal, and he clenched his jaw and scowled when he noted how some of them had suffered. In the worst shape of all was Trouble. David carefully applied to each wound an ointment of oil mixed with herbs. It took him almost an hour to tend to the whole flock.

"We'll stay close by today," he announced when he finished. "I think we all need to take it easy."

Hugo couldn't agree more.

They left the sheepfold with David in the lead. The sheep had returned to their wandering ways, forcing the shepherd to resort to flinging stones to keep them together. As promised, they didn't go far, stopping nearby in a newly harvested field of grain. In no time, the flock was happily grazing on the remaining stubble and new shoots.

Hugo figured now was as good a time as any to question David about Julia's theory.

"What town is this?" He pointed to a nearby hill. He hadn't noticed any signs of civilization before.

"Don't you know? It's Bethlehem, where I live."

At the sound of that name, Hugo became alarmed. It couldn't be the same Bethlehem from all the Christmas carols, could it? Were they really locked up in a Bible story? Hugo bit his lip. He then remembered Bethlehem still existed in the twenty-first century, so this didn't prove anything. Besides, there could be many different towns with the same name.

"If you told us more about where we are, maybe it could jog our memory," he suggested.

David shrugged. "What can I say? You're in the land of Judah in Israel. Go north, and you'll come to the tribe of

Benjamin, where King Saul lives. To our east is the Salt Sea. A day's journey to the west will bring you to the Philistines, our enemies whom you've had the pleasure of meeting."

His reply made Hugo even more nervous. He decided on a different line of questioning.

"Tell us about your latest technology," he asked.

"What do you mean?" David cocked his head.

"What are the latest weapons?"

"Ah. The best swords are made of iron, but unfortunately, the Philistines are better at making them than we are." He spat in disgust.

David's answer made a chill surge all over Hugo's body. If iron was the latest discovery, how far back in time would they be? He couldn't remember. History wasn't his thing, and he had rarely paid attention to details in school.

"Now it's my turn to ask questions," the shepherd said. "I don't believe for a second you've lost your memory. What are you really doing here?"

All three kids looked at him with such sadness that he took a step back in astonishment and scrutinized their faces for a minute without saying a word.

Julia marched right up to David. "We were at home minding our own business, and the next thing we know, we woke up here and you found us."

"We're looking for answers just as much as you are," Hugo said.

David studied them. Hugo felt as if the shepherd was trying to read their minds.

"Okay, so maybe I'll believe you after all." He waved his hand. "The Lord will sort it out."

The conversation died down. Hugo was beginning to believe Julia's theory was correct, but how could they return to their world if it was true? If looking at the old Bible triggered some mysterious mechanism to bring them here, how could they activate it again to take them home?

They sat in silence. David left to round up a few sheep that had wandered too far away, then returned and lay down.

"I bet you're popular back in Bethlehem," Hugo commented.

David sat up and looked at him blankly. "What do you mean? You three never cease to say the strangest things." He shook his head.

Hugo's face suddenly felt hot. "I mean, you must have lots of friends."

The shepherd's countenance darkened. "No, I don't." He had an unfocused gaze as if reliving something in his mind. "I've never been—what did you say? Popular. Quite the contrary."

Hugo stared at him, stunned. In his eyes, David was the embodiment of cool—tall, muscular, and confident. The shepherd would probably be a star athlete and part of the in-crowd if he went to Hugo's school. Hugo couldn't conceive of someone like David having friend problems. For a wimpy kid like himself, such issues were expected. For David the Super Jock? Impossible!

"I don't understand," Hugo continued. "You're the most courageous guy I've ever met. Every boy I know would look up to you. And every girl would fall in love with you too."

David laughed. Were his cheeks turning pinkish? "I wish what you said were true, but I've never had many friends. My brothers have made sure of that."

"I don't have any friends in my new school," Hugo admitted. When he realized what he had said, he froze. Would David turn on them now, trying to force out the truth of who they were by any means necessary? It was getting harder and harder to feign amnesia. The shepherd looked at him with a puzzled expression on his face.

"You three are so weird," he finally conceded. "It's as if you were from a different world."

If only you knew! Hugo bit his lip. He certainly couldn't admit to the truth. *Yes, we've come from thousands of years in the future.* He was sure David would have them committed to the ancient equivalent of an insane asylum.

"How do you cope with the loneliness?" Julia asked.

David flashed her the hint of a smile. "I talk to my sheep and remind myself the Lord is with me."

"I should have guessed your answer." She shook her head. "Whatever works for you."

David raised an eyebrow as he scrutinized her face. He then went to corral several more wandering animals. He disappeared for a few minutes before coming back to sit nearby.

Suddenly, Julia let out an ear-shattering scream. She jumped to her feet and turned white, pointing to a spot behind her brother. "Move. Now!"

Hugo couldn't see what she was pointing at, but the fear in her voice and the terror in her eyes convinced him to do as she said. He and Stefan joined her in one leap and looked in the direction of her horrified stare. There, lying right behind where they had been sitting, was a hideous snake.

David was calmly perched on a rock, unmoving like a stone. The three looked at him expectantly, hoping he would make a move to save them from this dreadful creature. Instead, his face distorted in an attempt to hide a smile. He finally gave up the fight and let out such a hearty laugh he had to clutch his stomach. They gaped at him in surprise, and it took a few seconds before they finally understood what had happened.

"You put it there, didn't you?" Julia glared. David couldn't answer because he was still in stitches. When he eventually calmed down, he shot them a guilty smile.

"I couldn't resist." His beaming grin betrayed a lack of remorse. "Don't worry. It's dead. I made sure," he added as if it was justification for the deed.

"I could have had a heart attack," Julia cried out. "I'm terrified of snakes."

Hugo could tell she didn't see the humor in the situation as he did. "You got us good," he chuckled.

"This is the best prank I've ever witnessed." Stefan was glowing. "I wish I had done it."

One look at his sister wiped the smile off his face. She was highly offended and ensured everyone could see it by the number of daggers shooting out of her eyes.

David glanced at the two boys and shrugged. "I thought a little humor would do us some good. Lighten the mood. Besides, it's my way of showing I've accepted you."

"How is a snake supposed to do that?" Julia stood with her hands on her hips. She still glowered at David.

"Well, I appreciate your gesture," said Hugo. "It's like an olive branch, isn't it?"

David gaped at him. "What do olives have to do with this?" He shook his head. "Another one of your crazy sayings."

"It's a symbol for making peace." When he saw David's frown, he quickly added, "Never mind."

"Where did you get it?" Stefan asked, approaching the dead reptile and timidly poking it with his foot.

"On the other side of the field. I saw it while I was checking on the sheep."

David picked up the snake and went to dump it somewhere far away. Stefan was right behind him.

Hugo watched them retreat. An unasked question had been burning inside him all day, but he hadn't dared bring it up. He decided to go for it when the shepherd returned.

"Why don't you ever get scared?"

David burst out laughing, which was not the response Hugo had expected. He felt his face flushing.

"Of course, I get scared. Where did you get such a crazy idea?"

Hugo gulped. "Because you don't show it. You didn't hesitate to fight the lion and take on those raiders."

"I *was* afraid when I saw the lion. Same with the raiders, but I didn't listen to my fears."

"But how can you ignore your fears so easily?" Hugo questioned.

David's eyes softened as he studied the boy. "Because they lie to us. Long ago, I decided to listen to another voice, the voice of my Lord. I guess it's a matter of trusting God more than my fears."

"It can't be so simple," Hugo shot back. "The lion could have killed you, and your fear wasn't lying then. The danger was real."

"You're right, but the lie wasn't about the danger. It wanted me to think the situation was hopeless and I was too weak to fight, so I better not even try. Had I listened, the lion would have surely killed us all."

Hugo was troubled. David's answer only convinced him even more of his own cowardice.

The shepherd eyed him with compassion. "Listen, I know it's not easy. I'm often terrified, too, but little by little, my courage has grown with each test of faith. Whatever bravery I have comes from knowing the Lord is with me and choosing to believe him." He walked over to Hugo and patted him on the back. "Don't worry. You'll find your courage."

A radiant smile formed on Hugo's face as hope flowed into his heart.

The rest of the day went by uneventfully, and Julia slowly got over her pouting. The sun had started its descent under the horizon when they began their trek back to the sheepfold.

Upon arriving, they had their evening meal—the same as they had had for breakfast. Hugo wasn't complaining, but a little variety would have been nice. They had eaten nothing else since arriving in this strange world.

Before long, they were sitting in a circle listening to David play his harp, mesmerized yet again.

"The way you describe God, it's as if you know him," Julia said when the music stopped.

"I write about my experience and how the Lord has worked in my life."

"But how can you know he's real?" she asked. "It's not like you can see him."

The shepherd examined her in silence. He hesitated for a long time before answering. "Let me give you an example. It's like with my uncle, Simon. I never met him because he died before I was born, but I've heard all about him from those who knew him, and I played with his sons as a child. So I know he exists even though I never saw him with my own eyes. It's the same with God. Sure, I've never seen him, but there's proof of his existence everywhere I look. Take the stars, for example." David pointed to the sky. "Who put them there?"

"Some cosmic event could have made the universe without divine help."

"Really? You think this universe could come into being on its own?" His mouth dropped open, and he rubbed his forehead. "Let me give you another reason why I believe in God. He's always taken good care of me. How could I ever deny he exists?"

Hugo pondered David's words. He had never given much thought to the existence of God before coming on this strange adventure.

"Have you always believed?" Hugo asked.

"My parents taught me about him, but it's here, out with the sheep, where I've come to know him. I distinctly remember the first night I was alone with the flock. I was about seven or eight, and I was terrified. I was sure robbers would attack me, and I got myself so worked up with fear I couldn't stop shaking. Finally, in desperation, I prayed. It was the simple prayer of a child, but the Lord heard me. I can't explain it, but peace enveloped me, and I felt as if God himself was holding me in his arms. And then my father appeared out of nowhere. He didn't say a word and sat down next to me. I was sure the Lord had sent him, and right then and there, I decided I could trust God and follow him."

A thought came to Hugo, and he sat straight up. "You know, if you're correct about God, then he's just like you are with your sheep. I see how much you care for them and everything you do, even risking your life. And you say God is the same way. It's as if he was your shepherd or something."

David was silent for a few seconds, absorbing his words. "You're right." His face lit up, and his eyes sparkled in the moonlight. "God does behave as any good shepherd would. Why didn't I think of it before?" He slapped Hugo on the back. "You've just given me the topic for my next poem."

It's time to hit the hay, or should I say, hit the sheepskins. Hugo smiled to himself at his lame joke. *I must be exhausted.*

They all stood and headed to their respective beds. It didn't take long for Hugo to hear David's rhythmic breathing nearby. Somewhere in the mystical land between wakefulness and slumber, the visions of his nightmares returned, and he drifted off to sleep with a sense of dread.

CHAPTER SEVEN

OFF TO BETHLEHEM

David shook Hugo. "Get up, sleepyhead." The boy yawned but quickly obeyed, one eye stuck closed. *I'm definitely going to sleep in late when I get home*. He swallowed hard, suddenly wide awake. *If I get home*.

The shepherd disappeared into the cave and reemerged with two sleepwalkers following him. He set out breakfast before them.

"Maybe you'll finally have the guts to try this?" David held out a chunk of the blackened and shrunken dried fish and waved it within an inch of Hugo's face.

The boy's stomach churned, and he thought he might lose it. "Um, maybe not for breakfast."

David turned towards the siblings, who shrunk back when he dangled the fish in front of them.

"It's tasty, you know, and good for you too." The shepherd chuckled at their reaction, then took a big bite.

They were still eating when David abruptly jumped to his feet and grabbed his staff. They could hear the sound of footsteps fast approaching. David attached his rod to his belt and felt for his leather pouch with the stones. Hugo and the siblings waited, barely remembering to breathe. Hugo could feel the tension in the air.

"David!" A friendly voice rang out in the faint dawn light.

"Abdon!" David yelled. He ran to the doorway to remove the big rock blocking the entrance. Two men stepped into the sheepfold.

The first to enter was short and middle-aged, followed by a tall, heavyset man holding a shepherd's staff. David gave both men a bear hug.

When the visitors appeared, Julia, Stefan, and Hugo got to their feet. David introduced the older man. "This is Abdon, my father's servant."

All three kids nodded. Hugo was stunned. *David's family has servants? How can he casually mention this fact—as if it's normal? He definitely didn't strike me as rich.*

"And this is Jonah, a shepherd who sometimes works for my family."

Hugo instinctively reached out to shake the men's hands. They stood motionless and stared, perplexed, at the boy's extended arm. After a few awkward seconds, Hugo quickly withdrew his hand in confusion. He stared down at his feet, unsure of what to do next.

"Your father has an errand for you," Abdon said. "He sent us to get you, and Jonah will stay behind to watch the sheep."

David's eyes sparkled. "What does he want me to do?"

"He didn't say. All we know is he wants you home as quickly as possible. So please, sir, we should be heading back."

David turned to his three guests and flashed them a beaming smile.

"You're going to Bethlehem with me. Maybe being in a city will help your memory come back."

All three faces turned pallid, and Hugo's mouth went dry.

David paused to give Jonah instructions, who nodded as if listening intently, but his gaze was far away. He looked like someone who had gone through this little routine many times and was bored to death. He leaned on his staff and tapped his toes, nodding absent-mindedly at David's words.

"This one here always gives us problems," David said, petting Trouble. "She saved the lives of Stefan and Julia, so be kind to her."

Jonah raised an eyebrow but didn't say a word.

They were soon on their way. Hugo felt a strange excitement. He was curious to see what a town looked like in this strange world, but the thought of leaving behind the friendly confines of the sheepfold made his heart race. He couldn't believe that the sheepfold had become a sort-of home for him in such a short time. Since they had no idea how to behave in this society, the more people they talked to, the greater the chance of doing something stupid and getting into trouble.

The trip to Bethlehem took no more than thirty minutes. On the way, they passed fields bustling with agricultural activity despite the early hour. They came to the foot of a hill, and Hugo looked up. When he saw the small town nestled on the top and encircled by a wall, he took a deep breath. Their path led straight to the gate. As they ascended, they passed terraced vineyards and olive groves covering the slopes.

When they entered the town, Hugo looked around, and the scene before him was stranger than he could have ever imagined. Any lingering doubts about being in ancient Israel disappeared. He finally had to admit that Julia was right.

As he scanned the town, he saw animals everywhere. Sheep, goats, and geese were all over the place. Everywhere he stared, he spotted donkeys pulling carts, bearing loads, or carrying people.

Everyone was wearing tunics, both men and women. Hugo openly gaped at the opulent embroidery of some of the clothes he saw or recoiled at the rags which sometimes passed for clothing.

No matter how hard he searched, he found no evidence of technology of any kind. From the many people carrying jugs, Hugo guessed modern amenities like running water weren't exactly a common occurrence. *Not good.* He sighed unhappily. He had secretly hoped for a shower.

A smell hung in the air, and he instinctively wrinkled his nose. It was like being on a sweltering bus full of unwashed passengers—with the windows closed. He made a move to pinch his nostrils but stopped himself in time. He might get a few dirty looks.

The streets were narrow and crowded, and as they walked, Hugo had the impression the houses on both sides were closing in on them. The buildings were square or rectangular with flat roofs and were crammed together, often sharing a wall.

The small group slowly made their way up the hill, and David paused sporadically to greet a passerby. The shepherd wiped the sweat trickling down from his forehead into his eyes.

They finally stopped before a house and knocked on the arched wooden door. After a few seconds, it opened. Hugo held his breath.

"You're here!" A tall, beautiful woman wrapped David in her arms. Black curly hair with streaks of gray peeked out from under her shawl. After a few seconds, she released him. Her sparkling brown eyes revealed the kindness in her soul.

"Uncle David!" A young girl squealed and jumped into his arms so quickly that he almost let her fall to the ground. She was laughing, and he smiled back. "Want to play Soldiers and Philistines with me?" she asked expectantly.

"Not now, Sarah." He put her down and patted her on the head.

David quickly introduced his mother and niece. Hugo and the siblings nodded shyly. They entered a small courtyard, which they crossed to enter the house. Abdon left them to attend to his work.

It took a few seconds for Hugo's eyes to adapt to the darkness. The only light source besides the open door was a small window with no glass. When Hugo's eyes adjusted, he noticed the space was divided by pillars and low brick walls into four parts: three side-by-side parallel rooms of the same length, with a long perpendicular section in the back. Most of the area was used for storage, with clay jars of all shapes and sizes lined up in neat rows like soldiers in formation. A large assortment of strange-looking wooden tools hung on the walls. David later explained they kept the flock in these rooms during the winter months and pointed out the empty feeding troughs in both back corners.

They climbed up a ladder that led to an opening in the ceiling. The second-floor layout was identical to the first, except the central room was open, creating a courtyard. Another ladder led to the roof, where there was one more room. The rest of the space was unused, and a wooden ledge ran all around the side to protect against falling.

A distinguished-looking man with a white beard to rival Santa Claus stepped out from one of the rooms. He lit up with a big smile.

"Father!" David yelled and rushed over to hug him.

"Thanks for coming so quickly," the old man exclaimed. "And who do we have here?" He eyed his three unexpected guests. This time they bowed.

"These are wandering travelers who need help to find their way home," the shepherd introduced them. "They showed up out of the blue and completely confused. They say they've lost their memory, so you'll have to forgive them for any strange behavior," he added, winking in their direction.

David's father invited the three to sit on cushions on the floor and offered them dried figs and water. Hugo gratefully drank and felt revitalized. They soon learned the rest of the household was busy working in the vineyards, olive groves, or fields, and even little Sarah was helping her grandmother. They sat, with nothing to do, for what seemed like forever. Hugo had never before felt so totally out of place.

Two of David's brothers and their families lived in the house, while the others were next door. His two sisters were married and had moved out. David disappeared with his father into his parents' room, and after a short time, he reemerged, looking thoughtful. He came to check on his guests.

"Where's your room?" Stefan asked.

"I'm up there on the roof," he said. "You'll sleep there tonight. I'm going back to the sheepfold today. Father said you could stay here while I'm gone."

Julia and Stefan gasped, while Hugo felt as if a bomb had just exploded inside of him. "Bring us with you on your errand!" he pleaded.

"I can't. It's too dangerous," David explained. "And besides, I won't be longer than two days. You'll be perfectly fine here. My parents will take good care of you."

"Then take us back to the sheepfold, and we can wait for you there," Julia begged.

"We'll behave, I promise," Stefan added.

Hugo worried that if they stayed in Bethlehem, they would eventually say or do something to draw unwanted attention—the kind that gets you into trouble. "I'd prefer to be at the sheepfold. And besides, we don't want to be a burden on your parents."

David hesitated. They nervously waited for his answer.

"Okay, you can come back with me, but you must stay there until I return. Understood?"

All three kids nodded eagerly.

David disappeared down the ladder. A few minutes later, Hugo followed him. He needed to go to the bathroom. When he got to the door leading to the courtyard, he saw David talking to his mother. He held back in the darkness of the room and listened.

"You better change your clothes while you're here. Your cloak is filthy."

"Mom!"

"Okay, okay. Do as you wish," she sighed. "But please stay for dinner. I'm making your favorite—lentil stew."

David smiled. "Thanks, Mom, but I prefer to go as soon as possible."

Hugo's heart sank. His mouth watered at the thought of something other than olives, figs, and the tortilla-looking bread.

"Think about your guests. I'm sure they would appreciate a warm meal."

Yes, you know it! Hugo instantly liked David's mom.

The shepherd threw up his arms in surrender. "Okay, you win."

Hugo inwardly rejoiced. *Yay!*

"Has anything interesting happened recently other than having guests?" she asked.

Long pause. "Not really."

What? Hugo's eyes became as big as dried figs. *What about the lion? And the raiders?* It then occurred to him he had often been just as secretive with his own mom. He felt a pang of guilt.

David's mother looked at him suspiciously as if she knew teenage sons weren't exactly forthcoming with information. "Have you written any more poems?"

David's eyes lit up, and he gladly recited some of his recent creations. His mother beamed as she listened to his words, but a frown quickly wrinkled her features. The verses were about pain and suffering. She remained silent after he finished speaking.

"Have they hurt you so much?" she finally asked, her voice trembling. David looked away from her. She took a step towards him and extended her arms to hug him but stopped herself at the last moment when she saw his scowl.

"When did your brothers put gall in your food?" she asked, referring to one of the verses he had recited.

"What does it matter?" He jerked his head backward. "It's only one of many things they've done."

This admission mortified her. "Why didn't you come to us?"

"And be accused of being a snitch? I prefer to suffer in silence than be a tattletale."

Her eyes filled with tears. "I'm so sorry, my dear son," she said softly. They were silent for a few seconds. David paced back and forth.

Hugo felt guilty about eavesdropping, but he couldn't pull away.

"They do love you, you know," she whispered. David looked at his mother, doubt evident upon his face.

"I'm not so sure." He turned and headed towards the door.

Hugo panicked. David was coming his way. He had no time to hide, so he stepped out into the courtyard.

David was startled, and his eyes narrowed as he glared at Hugo with suspicion. "What are you doing here?"

"I—I came to look for you." Hugo glanced over at David's mother and attempted a casual smile. He then leaned over to whisper in the shepherd's ear. "Where can I go to relieve myself?"

David did a double take, and then he burst out laughing.

The rest of the afternoon went by at an agonizingly slow pace. Hugo was sick and tired of sitting on cushions in the upper courtyard. His muscles ached, and he often stood up to stretch and get feeling back into his legs. He longed for a comfortable couch to lounge on. And a phone with Wi-Fi. And a cold glass of iced tea with tons of ice. Anything to distract from this endless waiting.

He couldn't stop thinking about the conversation he had overheard. He was stunned to learn of David's abuse at the hands of his brothers. Hugo felt an odd comfort and peace, knowing he wasn't the only one who had suffered the pain of rejection. David knew how it felt too. Hugo was surprised and impressed that the shepherd hadn't let the mistreatment weaken him. No one would guess what he had gone through by looking at him. *Unlike me.* He hung his head in shame. He had allowed self-pity and fear to rule his heart. *If David can be strong, then so can I.* He tried to encourage himself with these words but was filled with doubt instead.

David was busy making arrangements for his errand. When he came back to join the three, Hugo immediately noticed the shepherd was wearing a new, clean cloak and possibly a different tunic as well. Hugo chuckled silently. *Moms—they haven't changed.*

When it was finally dinnertime, the rest of the family returned. The first to climb the ladder was a tall man who had the build and jawline of a movie star.

"My goodness! His Majesty himself!" he said mockingly when he saw David. He was about to make another comment when he noticed the three guests and held his tongue. A woman followed him, and then another couple. The man reminded Hugo of a lumberjack—he was tall, well-built, and sported a long beard.

David introduced his two brothers and sisters-in-law. Hugo observed their behavior closely. *They're not even happy to see him,* he noted with sadness. The shepherd didn't seem to care or notice. *David must be used to such treatment.*

The women brought out a rug and put it on the floor. Everyone sat around on cushions or mats, and David's mother placed before them a large dish that smelled like heaven compared to what he had been eating. Hugo salivated thinking about his first hot meal since arriving in this ancient world.

The women gave everyone a small bowl. David discreetly showed Hugo, Stefan, and Julia how to proceed. Thanks to his kind gesture, they knew they should use the flatbread to scoop up the food. Hugo didn't hesitate to chow down. His first mouthful sent him to culinary heaven. Every bite gave his taste buds a reason to celebrate, although the stew's flavors were unlike anything he had ever tried.

Why did people bother to invent silverware? Hugo wondered. After all, hands were perfectly fine utensils for eating.

Despite the delicious food, the atmosphere during dinner was tense. One of the brothers—the movie star— looked at David, scowling. "Why are you here? Won't the sheep miss you?" he smirked.

"I sent for him." Their father gave the brother a stern look.

"He doesn't need a reason. After all, he lives here," their mother added. Her eyes moistened.

In the middle of the meal, David's brothers showed interest in the three guests.

"So tell me, where are you from exactly?" Movie Star asked Hugo. His tone sounded like a police detective interrogating a suspect.

"I've already told you, they don't remember," David interjected.

"I'm asking him, not you."

Hugo glanced over at the siblings for emotional support. He didn't dare look the intimidating brother in the eye. "We just woke up here one day. We have no idea what happened, how we got here, or how to return home."

"Oh, my!" he answered sarcastically. "And what in the world could have caused such a strange predicament?"

Hugo swallowed hard. "As I said, sir, we don't know." He lifted his head to peep at the interrogating brother and saw dark, fiery eyes glaring back at him.

"Leave them alone. Can't you see they're still traumatized?" David said.

"You stay out of this! You bring them into my house, and I don't even think they're Israelites. They're probably spies. The land has been crawling with them since the Philistines attacked."

"Do you doubt my judgment?" There was a challenge in David's voice.

"As a matter of fact, we do," said Lumberjack.

"Enough, you three!" their father cried out.

"Mark my words, I'll get to the bottom of their story!" Movie Star warned. "There's something fishy about them."

"How dare you be so rude to our guests." The father glared at both of David's brothers. "Where are your manners? I didn't raise you to be so impolite." He then turned towards all three kids. "Please accept my apologies for their behavior."

Hugo and the siblings nodded timidly.

The brothers didn't say another word, but their eyes burned as they stared at Julia and Stefan with crooked smiles.

A cold shiver slithered up and down Hugo's spine, and panic took over his thoughts. It suddenly hit him why David's brothers terrified him so much—they reminded him of the bullies from school. He folded his arms to keep them from trembling, but he could still feel himself shake. He desperately wanted to escape this ancient world if only he could figure out how to go home.

None of the men spoke for the rest of the meal. David's mother and sisters-in-law tried to lighten the mood without success. When everyone finished eating, they wiped their bowls with the bread and turned them upside down. Julia, Stefan, and Hugo promptly followed suit.

Once everyone stood up, Lumberjack sneaked up behind Hugo and whispered, "Just wait till David is gone. We're coming for you. You may have fooled our wide-eyed brother, but you can't fool us." He glared at him with an icy smile.

Hugo stood frozen until David grabbed his arm and declared it was time to leave. The sun was about to set. The shepherd waited for his guests to climb down the ladder before doing so himself. Back in the courtyard, Abdon helped David load a donkey heaping with provisions. Meanwhile, Hugo and the siblings huddled together in one of the corners.

"We'll never be safe in this world. We have to get back home soon!" whispered Hugo.

"I know, but how?" Julia asked.

"It's a good thing we're not staying in Bethlehem," Stefan muttered.

"Don't you get it? The sheepfold won't protect us." Hugo nervously looked around to make sure he wouldn't be overheard. "David's brothers are convinced we're spies. One of them warned me they're coming for us."

"When?" both Julia and Stefan asked simultaneously.

"When we stood up from the meal."

As if on cue, Movie Star and Lumberjack poked their heads out the door. They glared at the three youths, then hastily retreated into the house.

"David, hurry up!" Julia whispered. She was quivering.

"Time to go!" the shepherd announced.

It took every ounce of self-control for Hugo not to book it to the gate. He looked back at the door to the house. It shifted ever so slightly, revealing the faint outline of a silhouette.

They stepped out into the street and walked down the hill in silence. Only when they left Bethlehem behind did Hugo feel his body begin to relax.

"We'll miss you while you're gone!" Stefan said. "What're you going to do?"

"I'm bringing provisions to my other brothers on the front lines. I'll leave first thing in the morning. Father doesn't want me to travel alone at night."

"Front lines of what?" Stefan cried out. "Is there a war?"

David stopped walking and eyed the boy in surprise. "Don't you know?" A look of recognition crossed his face. "Of course, how could I forget? You've lost your memory. Well, the Philistines attacked us. Who else?"

They continued down the path in silence.

"Why did your brother call you 'His Majesty'?" Stefan blurted out.

Doesn't this guy have any boundaries? Hugo cringed.

David looked at Stefan in stunned silence, and a few minutes went by before he answered.

"Maybe it's finally time to talk about it. Get it off my chest," the shepherd mumbled to himself. "I've never mentioned this to anyone. What I'm about to tell you must remain between us. Understood?"

All three nodded vigorously.

"My brothers never really cared for me because I'm the youngest, but something happened to make them hate and resent me." A pained look came upon his face.

The kids waited for him to continue.

"Several years ago, the prophet Samuel came to Bethlehem. He invited my father and brothers to join him, but I was away with the sheep, so I didn't know about it. Suddenly, Jonah showed up at the sheepfold and told me to hurry home, wash, and change before going to my father. I was intrigued and quickly did as instructed. When I arrived where they were, I could tell something strange was happening. I couldn't believe I was in the presence of the great prophet Samuel. and I thought my knees would buckle. My brothers were standing to the side. If looks could kill, I would've been dead on the spot. Their gazes were so piercing I had to turn away. Father was next to them, totally bewildered." David paused for a moment, staring into the distance.

"Before I knew what was happening, Samuel approached me. He told me to kneel. I was surprised, but I wasn't about to argue with him, so I obeyed. He took the ram's horn in his hand, lifted it over me, and poured the oil on my head, proclaiming me to be the next king of Israel. At first, I was numb. It didn't register what he was doing. All I could feel was the oil running down my head. But when I realized what had happened, I felt like a thousand arrows hit me simultaneously, and I started shaking. Samuel had to help me back to my feet. When I stood up, I felt a strange power fill every part of my body, and I could barely keep myself from running around and screaming."

David's listeners gawked at him, speechless.

"The worst part was my brothers' resentment. It was so strong it bore a hole in my soul," he continued. "They acted as if I was behind it all, as though I had convinced the prophet to choose me somehow, but believe me, no one was more shocked than I was!"

"Why are you in the fields with the sheep and not in a castle ruling the nation?" Stefan exclaimed.

"For a long time, I pondered what to do. It's not something we talked about in my family. We never even mentioned it again, other than my brothers sometimes calling me 'His Majesty' to mock me. We were all terrified of being overheard. If King Saul ever found out, he would kill me and the rest of my family while he's at it."

David stopped walking. He took hold of his staff with both hands and leaned on it, closing his eyes. "I fought with the Lord, wondering why he chose me." He opened them again and looked straight ahead. "I was sure he had made a mistake. I mean, I'm a nobody! I'm nothing but a shepherd. I love being out with the sheep, playing the harp, and writing poems—hardly king material. I prayed and prayed about what to do, and it's now clear I must wait. The Lord will bring it about in his own time."

"Can't you simply tell the king that God has chosen you, and he should step down?" Stefan pressed further.

David laughed so hard that he let go of his staff. When he recovered, he leaned forward to pick it back up. "That's not how it works! Where would you even get such a crazy idea?" He was still chuckling when he continued. "Don't you know death is the only means of succession? I would have to kill Saul." He turned serious. "But I can't have his blood on my hands. God has told me in no uncertain terms. Since the Lord chose me, he is strong enough to make me king. He doesn't need me to try to help him by doing something stupid."

They resumed walking. It dawned on Hugo that modern democracy has not been the norm for most of human history. The ancient world knew nothing about the peaceful transition of one leader to another. *I'm happy I don't live back in those days.* He caught himself. *Well, hopefully, I won't soon.* He sighed.

"So, you do nothing?" Stefan's jaw looked like it was stuck in the open position.

"No, I'm preparing to be the best king possible when the time comes. And besides," David said, grinning, "the Lord came up with an ingenious way to get me close to Saul, allowing me to observe and learn how a king behaves."

"What way?" Stefan leaned closer.

"I play my harp for him. Can you believe it?" David's eyes beamed.

"Why don't you talk to your brothers and explain it all to them?" Julia said.

"I've tried, but they won't listen. I've finally given up, and we go on as if nothing has happened. But all the emotions are still there, festering under the surface."

"I know what you mean about ignoring bad feelings," Julia said. "Our parents are always fighting." Her voice trailed off as a tear slipped from the corner of her eye. "They pretend everything is okay in front of us, but they don't realize we hear them yelling at night."

David looked over at her and then at her brother. Their pain was written all over their faces. "Can I recite something which helps me when I'm sad?"

They nodded.

David looked up at the sky. "The Lord is close to those whose hearts are broken. He saves those whose spirits are discouraged. A righteous man may have many a problem. But from every one of them, he is delivered."

He turned to face them. "God knows what you're going through. He's not indifferent to your suffering."

"Thank you." Julia's voice shook, and her eyes glistened.

They continued their trek in silence, deep in thought.

"So, your memory has come back!" David gave them a sly smile.

Julia flushed. "It's hard to forget such pain," she answered. She tried to grin at him, but her expression still reflected her anguish.

"Don't you sometimes feel like sticking it to your brothers?" Stefan asked. "I mean, don't you fantasize about getting back at them once you're the king?"

David laughed. "What do you think?" The spark in his eyes was all the answer they needed.

The conversation died down as they continued down the path in silence.

The hair on the back of Hugo's neck stood straight up when he remembered Lumberjack's threat. He imagined himself and his friends in shackles in a dark room with David's brothers using all means necessary to get them to confess that they were Philistine spies. *I've seen too many movies.* He tried unsuccessfully to shake the image from his mind. One thing was sure—David's brothers were coming for them, but what could they do? The more he thought about it, he knew that their only choice was to secretly follow David on his journey to deliver the provisions. He wasn't about to stay behind and fall victim to whatever scheme the brothers had concocted. *They're too much like the bullies from school.* Hugo wiped the sweat that poured down his forehead into his eyes.

When they arrived at the sheepfold, David joyfully greeted his sheep, who were just as happy to see him. In the moonlight, he briefly inspected every animal.

Jonah observed his actions, half-smiling. "I checked them out, you know," he said. He slapped David on the head.

"You know me. I can't help myself. It's nothing against you."

While the two shepherds were unloading the donkey, Hugo discreetly got the siblings' attention and whispered his conclusion about what they should do. Dismayed, they agreed with his plan. Following David into the unknown was scary enough, but staying behind to face his brothers was even more terrifying.

"It's getting late, and I have a busy day ahead of me tomorrow. Goodnight, everyone!" David announced before curling up on his sheepskins by the opening in the wall.

Julia and Stefan headed for the cave while Hugo lay down on his bed. He was determined to stay awake at all costs. The frightening road ahead of them loomed large. No matter where it led, they were compelled to follow.

CHAPTER EIGHT

WALKING INTO PERIL'S WAY

Hugo was stretched out on his sheepskin, fighting to keep his eyes open. He knew if they closed for even a second, sleep would engulf him faster than he could count to three. The night dragged on, and staying awake was getting harder and harder. When his eyelids became so heavy he was sure tiny barbells weighed them down, David finally stirred. The shepherd got up and was careful not to make a noise as he crept about the sheepfold. He quickly loaded up the donkey.

Hugo lay still to avoid causing any suspicion while monitoring David's movements. He wondered if the siblings were asleep when he caught sight of Stefan peeking out from the cave entrance. Hugo's pulse quickened, hoping the shepherd hadn't noticed.

The time to leave had come. David looked over at his sheep, and the corners of his mouth lowered. "Why do I feel as if I'll never see you again?" he whispered to his flock. Even in the moonlight, Hugo could notice the reflection of tears filling the shepherd's eyes.

David approached each animal and gently patted it on the head. When he came to Trouble, he paused, leaned over to kiss her, and hugged her for a few seconds. Standing back up, he wiped away a tear, grabbed his staff, took hold of the donkey, and walked out of the sheepfold without looking back.

Hugo sprung to his feet while Julia and Stefan dashed out of the cave. They raced for the entrance, only to come face-to-face with Jonah. He looked down at them, smirking.

"We need to relieve ourselves," Hugo whispered. He was anxious to get going.

"All three at the same time?" the shepherd asked, with a crooked smile, clearly amused.

"Yes," came the feeble reply.

Jonah looked at them and crossed his arms. Hugo was growing antsier by the second. He thought about forcing his way out, but the man was too tall and bulky. Finally, the shepherd moved aside to let them go. They rushed through the opening before he could change his mind.

For a second, Hugo panicked. He couldn't see where David had gone. He scanned the horizon and exhaled when he saw him and the donkey in the distance. The moon cast just enough light to make everything visible.

They set out. David was following a path along an unbroken ridge. Hugo was thankful they were steadily going downhill. Otherwise, he would have been huffing and puffing. Even so, they had difficulty keeping up with David's brisk pace. The shepherd was in a hurry and didn't stop to rest even once. Despite their best effort, the distance between them gradually expanded.

"Let's run a bit to catch up," Hugo whispered to the siblings when David disappeared around a bend. They took off along the rocky and uneven path, but Hugo's sandals slipped on the loose pebbles, sending him flying, and he landed with a thud. He lay immobile, feeling sorry for himself, when it suddenly hit him. *My nightmare! I'm in the scene from my first dream.* He saw himself running in the wilderness after a shadowy figure. Panicked, his chest constricted, and he found it difficult to breathe. He paused and forced his lungs to inhale. *Will my second dream—with that muscular thug chasing me—come true, too?* He didn't want to dwell on the answer and pushed the thought out of his mind. He could do nothing about it anyway, other than be vigilant. He got back on his feet and trembled.

The sky grew lighter, meaning the sunrise was not too far away. When David came back in sight, Hugo felt much more exposed and worried the shepherd would see them if he glanced their way. They might not have time to hide behind the trees and bushes scattered here and there or the large rocks adorning the countryside.

The sun finally peeked over the ridge. Hugo had no time to notice the beautiful colors in the sky and the fantastic display of light and shadow on the terrain. He also didn't detect the faint sound of footsteps, which could be heard once or twice behind them. Instead, he focused on their stealthy pursuit of David.

David abruptly turned around and looked straight in their direction as if suspecting something. Hugo and the siblings fell flat on the ground and closed their eyes tightly, hearts pounding. The undulation in the hillside hid them from sight. Several minutes went by before they dared to stand up again. When they did, the shepherd had disappeared.

They looked around distressed, then continued down the path. Whenever they went around a bend or over a crest, Hugo expectantly scanned the horizon, but David was nowhere in sight.

"I hope this is the right direction," Julia whispered.

"I can't imagine him going any other way," Hugo muttered. "I'm sure he's not too far ahead," he added, to reassure himself as much as her. The problem was, he didn't believe it.

"I'm starting to doubt we made the right decision following David," she said. Stefan nodded.

The landscape slowly changed to include more and more trees. Hugo beat himself up for taking his friends on this reckless journey. They might have been safe at the sheepfold after all. Maybe Movie Star and Lumberjack had just wanted to talk to them. Instead, they were wandering in a wilderness with no one to help.

Hugo glanced at the sky. *God? Um, are you there?* He paused, not knowing what to say. *We could really use your help. We're in trouble, and it's my fault. I don't know what to do.* He hoped someone was listening.

The further they walked, the more Hugo doubted they would ever see David again. They stumbled around a bend and froze.

Two men stood blocking their path and stared at them with an evil sneer. They looked like they had stepped straight out of a horror movie. Their large builds towered over the kids, and their tattered and torn clothes revealed powerful muscles. One carried a club, and a patch covered one of his eyes. The other was at least a foot taller and held a dagger. A single glance was enough to know they were fierce warriors.

"Your life has just taken a turn for the worst!" growled the largest of the men. When he lifted the blade in his hand, he let out a wicked laugh, making the gruesome scars disfiguring his face even more grotesque. His biceps were so huge he could easily be on the cover of a bodybuilding magazine in the modern world.

Those are the muscles from my second nightmare! Terror seized Hugo, and he felt nauseous.

All three kids turned to run back up the path, but two more men stood behind them, cutting off their escape. One held a club, while the other had an ax attached to his belt. They snickered.

Hugo felt someone grab him from behind and lift him a foot in the air. "Where do you think you're going?" the man whispered into his ear. He threw Hugo to the ground. "There's nowhere to hide, and your friend with the donkey is long gone. He'll never hear you scream."

Stefan helped Hugo back to his feet. The thugs closed in on the three kids like a noose. Hugo instinctively knew there was no point in fighting or pleading for mercy.

Without warning, the eye patch man grabbed Julia by the chin and jerked her head back, forcing her to look at him. He was pleased to see the terror in her eyes. His smirk revealed a pair of rotten teeth.

"You better be afraid," he sneered, pulling her closer.

"Leave her alone!" Stefan shouted. Nostrils flaring, he punched the robber in the torso with his right fist. The man threw Julia to the side and drilled Stefan in the chest, sending him crashing to the ground. He then stepped in the boy's direction and shrieked, grabbing his club.

"Watch out with the merchandise!" shouted the man with the ax. "They must be in good shape to fetch a reasonable price." He ran to place himself between Stefan and the eye patch man, whose face had turned red and spittle had built up in the corners of his mouth.

"How dare you tell me what to do!" Club in hand, he walked right up to the axman, who stood waiting for him, holding on tightly to his weapon.

"Enough!"

The thundering voice made everyone jump. The huge robber with the gruesome scars approached the two who had been arguing. He towered over them and pointed his dagger at each in turn. They dropped their heads and took a step backward.

The gigantic thief lowered his blade. "He's right. As much as I hate to admit it"—he spat a massive blob of saliva—"we need the money, and they won't be worth much if damaged. Keep your aggression for another day!"

The eye patch man squeezed his clenched fists but didn't move. "As you wish, Akar," he said.

Julia ran over to Stefan, still lying spread-eagle on the ground. She helped him to his feet and gave him a big hug, tears flowing down her face. Their tender moment was quickly interrupted by strong hands, who harshly pulled them apart and smacked them on the head.

"Start marching," Akar ordered as he pushed them down the path. "And don't try anything stupid. We won't be so merciful a second time."

They walked in silence. The robbers kept their prisoners in front of them to guard their every move. *As if we could run away,* Hugo scoffed inwardly. He burned with shame that he hadn't reacted like Stefan when the thug attacked Julia. Instead, he had stood there and done nothing—just like the snake incident in the river. Just like *the day. I'm such a chicken.* He tortured himself with those words over and over again.

Suddenly, the robbers grabbed Hugo and the siblings from behind. They brutally jerked them to the side of the road. Rugged and stinky hands covered their mouths, forcing the three to lie down on the ground behind the low branches and gnarled trunk of a terebinth tree. They held Hugo and the siblings so tightly they could barely breathe.

Voices echoed in the distance, and soon a man and a teenage boy were coming up the path. They were in a hurry and nervously glanced around in every direction as if suspecting danger.

Hugo watched them approach, feeling completely powerless and dejected when an unexpected thought flashed across his mind like an advertising banner pulled by a small plane. *What if my dreams were sent to me as a sign and were part of a larger plan?* If this was true, then someone other than the robbers was in control. Their predicament might not be as helpless as he had thought.

Suddenly, he saw himself and the last six months of his life with newfound clarity, as if he had put on a new, sharper pair of glasses. Ever since his move to Pennsylvania, he had let fear control his thoughts and actions. His anxiety had snuffed out all his bravery and courage. He had listened to its destructive message telling him to withdraw and shrink back, paralyzing him.

No wonder he reacted the way he did on *the day*. He let himself relive the scene for the first time since it happened.

He was walking home after classes when Dan, the meanest kid in school, jumped out from behind a tree and blocked his way. He was at least six inches taller than Hugo despite being in the same grade. Hugo turned around, only to come face to face with Dan's burly cronies, Dylan and Mark. Hugo didn't move and kept his eyes focused on the ground as they taunted him and slapped his head with increasingly greater force until it hurt. He furiously racked his brain to figure out a way of escape, but he came up blank. Panic grabbed hold of him, constricting his lungs and making breathing difficult.

"Stop it!"

Everyone turned in the direction of the shout. Hugo couldn't believe his eyes when he saw Sammy, his neighbor from down the street, march towards them, taking steps as big as his short, skinny legs would allow. When he was a few feet away, he stopped, crossed his arms, and stood as straight as possible, barely reaching Hugo's ears.

"Leave Hugo alone."

The bullies burst out laughing. "You think you can stop us? You're just a kid. Turn around and hurry home," Dan said.

"I'm not going anywhere."

Dylan strutted over to Sammy and shoved him to the ground, but the boy jumped back on his feet. The other two bullies circled around him.

Dan turned towards Hugo. "Get out of here."

Hugo froze. He wanted to stay to protect Sammy, but his fears took over. The scared voice in his head told him that he wasn't brave enough to fight. It told him to save himself, mocking him that he was too weak to help anyway. His heartbeat blasted off at light speed. And so he obeyed that voice full of fear. Spinning his legs as fast as possible, he bolted down the path, not looking back, not even when poor Sammy screamed. He didn't stop until he got home, rushed to his room, and dove under the blankets on his bed. He stayed there all evening, refusing to come down for dinner.

The next day, Sammy showed up at school with a black eye, telling everyone he ran into a tree. Hugo burned with shame and avoided the younger boy like he was radioactive. The guilt gnawed at his soul, destroying his self-esteem, and shredding his confidence. It cemented his view of himself as a coward and a loser.

Dan and his sidekicks took great pleasure in blackmailing Hugo for the rest of the school year. They threatened to reveal what happened unless he gave them his lunch, which he always did. To keep from starving, Hugo hid snacks in his backpack. He longed to be free from their clutches.

The sound of nearby footsteps jerked Hugo back to the present. He assessed his current situation—captured by ruthless thugs—and anxiety burned in his chest. For the first time in his life, he didn't cower behind his fear. *I don't have to listen to my fears.* This simple sentence set off a chain reaction within Hugo. A tiny ray of hope seeped into his soul. Could it be that he was not the chicken he thought he was? Was it possible he had merely been following the wrong voices? He had never before considered asking God for help, but Hugo finally understood what David had been trying to tell him—his courage came from above.

A plan solidified in Hugo's mind. He was going to be on the lookout for any opportunity to escape. Something was bound to happen, and when it did, he would pounce. Hugo watched the man and boy disappear while faith awoke in his heart.

His new attitude was immediately tested when the robbers violently yanked him back to his feet and pushed him down the path. Yet, he didn't waver in his determination.

"We have to get off the road!" Akar barked. "I know a shortcut so we can get to the Philistines as soon as possible. A guy in Gath can help us sell them." He glanced at the three and smiled maliciously.

Further west, David reached the camp of the Israelite army. He quickly found the supply tents to have his donkey unloaded and given food and water. As the attendants unpacked the animal's bags, a loud noise made David jump. It was the voices of thousands of men yelling at the top of their lungs, followed by metal banging on metal.

"What's that sound?"

"The army's going out to take its battle positions. They're shouting the war cry," the attendant answered.

"As if they will scare our enemy away!" a nearby man said.

"Tell me more," David asked. He moved closer to the speaker.

"Listen, we've been here for ages. Every day it's the same thing"—the soldier paused to spit—"we're on one side of the valley, and the Philistines are on the other. We sit and stare at each other as if we'll make the other army disappear." He spat again. "Every morning and evening, one of their soldiers challenges us to a duel, which no one accepts. We all return to our tents at night, only to repeat the same stupid process the next day. This charade has been going on for so many days I've lost count. I'm sick and tired of it."

David decided he wanted to see the action, and the sooner, the better. He hurried away from the supply tents, promising to come back for his donkey later, and ran in the direction of the noise. It wasn't hard to find the front lines. He searched for his brothers. Despite everything that had happened between them, part of him still looked forward to seeing them. He hoped for a warm reception but knew it was unlikely. Unfortunately, he was correct.

"What are you doing here?" his oldest brother asked forcefully when David found him.

"Nice to see you, too, Eliab," David responded, both disappointed and angry. "Father asked me to bring you supplies and to find out how you're doing. After all, you haven't bothered to send any word for over a month."

"How could we? We've been stuck here for what seems like forever."

A tense standoff followed, which was mercifully broken up by the arrival of David's second-oldest brother.

"David!" he cried out.

"Hi, Abinadab." Their greeting was friendlier. Just then, a third brother showed up. He went through the motions of a warm welcome but forgot to bring the warmth.

"So, what food did father send us?" Eliab asked. "I'm looking forward to something new. Army chow isn't exactly like Mom's home cooking."

"Some bread, cheese, and roasted grain."

"Nothing more? It's a shame you didn't bring any fig cakes," Abinadab lamented.

"I'll pass on the word," David said. "Any other special orders?" When no one answered, he continued, "So tell me, what's up? What should I tell Father?"

The three brothers glanced at each other. "There's not much to report. We guard this side of the valley, and the Philistines guard the other side. Our biggest enemy right now is boredom, not them." Eliab pointed in the direction of the enemy lines.

Abinadab chimed in. "I wish we would finally get to fight." He looked over at the Philistine positions across the valley. "They thought they could march to the Jordan River unopposed, but we've stopped them. I can't wait to push those losers all the way back to the sea."

Suddenly, a loud yell blasted on the valley's southern side, where the Philistine soldiers stood. They shouted and pounded their round shields with their swords. Their ranks abruptly opened up, and out from their midst emerged a two-horse chariot, which sprinted towards the valley. In the front, a driver masterfully directed the galloping animals. Behind him, a soldier was carrying an enormous shield. In the rear of the chariot stood the biggest man David had ever seen.

The chariot approached the middle of the valley. The Israelite soldiers who had wandered down the hill bolted back to the safety of their ranks. The horses halted, and silence descended upon the whole area as if time had come to a standstill. No one moved or said a word. David was utterly mesmerized as he watched the Philistine soldier step out of the chariot.

The mammoth warrior was so tall that even the horses looked tiny in comparison, barely reaching the man's shoulders. The shield-bearer, who took his place before the giant, looked like a child next to him. They walked closer to the Israelite position.

The Philistine oozed pride and arrogance. Scale armor covered his body, and he wore a helmet of bronze with a plume hanging from the top. His arms and legs were like tree trunks, and bronze shin guards protected his legs below the knees. A scabbard holding a huge sword was on his side, and a javelin was slung across his back. In one hand, he was carrying an enormous spear with an iron point so gigantic David was sure it required several normal-sized men to lift it.

The Israelites continued to be silent as they watched him approach. David could feel their terror. He was alarmed to realize this Philistine was causing so much fear in the hearts of his countrymen. Even his brothers were terrified, and he couldn't remember ever seeing them so frightened.

David moved closer to the front to get a better view. The giant stopped when he got close enough for the Israelites to hear him and looked at them with obvious disdain. As David observed the scene, anger rose within him. He was greatly offended at the contempt he could feel from the Philistine.

"Soldiers of Israel, why do you even bother lining up for battle?" the giant shouted. His voice was like the sound of thunder, and there was mockery in his tone. "Why should everyone fight and die unnecessarily? I am a Philistine, and I represent my people. You choose a man from among your ranks, O army of Saul. Let the two of us settle the matter together! If he can kill me," he sneered, "then we will become your slaves. But"—he spat—"if I kill him, then you will be subject to us. I defy the army of Israel to find a man brave enough, or foolish enough, to fight me!"

He glared at the soldiers on the hill and challenged them with his fiery gaze. His eyes radiated hatred. "I'll give you one hour, as usual." He smirked. "Will you continue to answer me with fear and cowardice?"

David looked down at the giant, and an idea formed in his mind. At first, it was only a whiff of a notion, but it quickly occupied all of his thoughts. While reflecting on this, a conversation nearby grabbed his attention.

"You would think this Philistine would have given up by now. He comes here day after day to challenge us, but no one would be foolish enough to fight him," one of the soldiers said.

"Don't you want the king's reward?" a young man asked.

"Hah! Of course, I do!" the first speaker said. "Who wouldn't want the money and the king's daughter in marriage? And never having to pay taxes ever again. All you have to do is fight a giant armed to the teeth. No big deal. Sign me up." His eyes narrowed. "If the king thinks he'll find any takers, he's a fool." He spat.

"I'd choose the money and no taxes over the daughter any day," a third warrior said.

The threesome moved on out of hearing range. David was burning with thoughts and emotions bouncing around in his mind. He didn't know who made him angrier—the Philistine giant who mocked the Israelite army or his compatriots who let him do it without reacting. What upset him the most was the lack of faith in God he was witnessing.

David approached another group of soldiers to verify the accuracy of the conversation he had overheard. "Tell me, what is the reward for the man who kills the Philistine and removes this dishonor from Israel?" His determination and sincerity startled the men.

"Are you joking?" one of them asked. "You're really thinking of fighting Goliath? Look at you! You're not even dressed like a soldier."

"What have my clothes got to do with anything? I'm dead serious." David was almost shaking. The rage within him had reached a boiling point. "Who does this pagan Philistine think he is? How dare he come here and defy the army of the living God? Doesn't he realize he's messing with the Lord Almighty Himself?" He glared at the soldiers. "And why don't you have the faith to fight him?"

The men looked at each other in shock. They didn't know what to make of this guy. They answered David's question about the reward, confirming what he had heard earlier, and then quickly moved on, clearly uncomfortable.

As David was standing and looking at the giant wondering what to do next, he noticed a growing number of curious onlookers surrounding him. Word must have been spreading about his inquiries into fighting the Philistine. Before long, his oldest brother appeared, as intrigued as everyone else to see who was asking about taking on the giant.

When Eliab saw his youngest sibling had caused all this commotion, he shook from rage. Shoving soldiers out of the way, he marched right up to David and looked him straight in the eye.

"What are you doing here, anyway?" he yelled. "Aren't you supposed to watch over your tiny flock of sheep out in the desert? Who's caring for them while you're gone? You better go back before they notice you're not there. They'll miss their beloved shepherd!" He was livid and bared his teeth. "How vain and wicked you are! You probably tricked Father into sending you. You just wanted to come and see the battle for yourself!"

"What have I done to deserve this?" David answered. "I was only asking some questions. Is that forbidden?" He wanted to throw his brother an uppercut but walked away before saying or doing something he would regret. It wouldn't be a good idea to come to blows in front of everyone. He breathed deeply and closed his eyes to calm his raging emotions and focus his thoughts. By the time he opened them again, his brother had disappeared.

The soldiers surrounding David gawked at him, speechless, causing him to feel uncomfortable. He turned his attention to Goliath, standing and talking to his shield-bearer. The Philistine sure looked intimidating. Nonetheless, the idea which appeared only a few minutes earlier had taken over his thoughts—he should fight this giant. Was this what the Lord wanted?

As was his habit when needing guidance, he prayed. The memory of a lion attack popped into his mind. The animal had scattered the flock and carried off one of the sheep. David ran after it and quickly caught up. He used his rod to hit the lion with such force that it let go of its prey. It turned around, gave a roar, and attacked. The shepherd grabbed its mane with one hand, and with the other, he struck it with the rod, killing it instantly.

As David pondered why he had this recollection, all his doubts about fighting Goliath evaporated. It had to be a sign. The Lord was telling him he would be victorious. If God could help him against such a frightening and powerful lion, he could certainly give him the strength to triumph over this terrifying giant.

"Excuse me, sir," a soldier interrupted his thoughts. "The king would like to see you," he announced. "Please follow me."

Wow, Lord, you work fast. David laughed inwardly, not surprised, and they set off. He spotted King Saul from a distance. The monarch was almost a foot taller than all the other men, and his royal clothes and armor distinguished him from those nearby.

When the king saw David, he jerked his head back. "Aren't you one of my armor-bearers?"

"Yes, Your Majesty." David bowed low. "It's been my pleasure to play my harp for you."

Saul nodded, a smile forming on his face. "Word has reached me that you're inquiring about fighting the giant."

"Yes, Your Majesty. Overhearing the troops, I can tell they are afraid and discouraged because of this Philistine, but they shouldn't be, My Lord! I, your servant, will go and fight him!" David looked up at the king with conviction.

Saul was quiet. He stared at the shepherd so intently that David thought the king was trying to read his mind. A few minutes went by as everyone waited for his response. David was growing fidgety.

"I don't think you can fight Goliath," Saul finally declared. "I admire your courage, I do, but look at you. You're only a boy, not a soldier.

David couldn't subdue the rising disappointment and distress within him. He had to convince Saul he could defeat the giant.

"Yes, while it's true that your servant has been a shepherd keeping my father's sheep, it doesn't mean I'm not a warrior." David chose his words carefully. "Maybe I haven't faced many soldiers in battle, but I've had combat of a different kind, and I've always come out victorious." His voice grew louder as he continued. "I've killed both lions and bears whenever they've attacked my sheep, and this Philistine will be like one of them because he has dared to come against the army of the living God!"

David's words rang out clearly and commanded the attention of the king, his entourage, and everyone within earshot. "You doubt me because you don't realize the source of my strength," he went on. "God is the one who gave me those victories, and for him, nothing is impossible. The Lord's the one who delivered me from the paws of the lion and the bear, and he will deliver me from the hand of Goliath. What is a giant to him?" David stopped and realized he was sweating all over. His fiery eyes dared Saul to keep him from fighting the Philistine.

The king looked conflicted. David lifted an urgent, silent prayer, pleading with the Lord to convince Saul to let him fight. After what felt like an eternity, the king looked over at one of his commanders, who nodded.

"Go and fight this Philistine," he finally said, "and may the Lord be with you."

David's emotions spilled in all directions like a smashed jar with its content flowing out. He felt euphoria and excitement, as well as fear and awe. *Lord, it's all up to you now.*

"If you're going to fight this giant, you must be dressed properly, like a soldier," Saul added. "Here, I will give you my armor to wear." He nodded to an attendant who disappeared and quickly returned, carrying one of the king's tunics and spare armor.

David inwardly balked at the idea but decided to give it a try. He didn't want to alienate the king and give him a reason to change his mind. First went on the tunic. David rolled up the sleeves feeling like a boy trying on his father's clothes, but before he could protest, the coat of armor was placed on him. He had never worn anything so heavy and uncomfortable. It was too big and impeded his arm movements. The attendant fastened it as tightly as possible, but it was still too broad and long. They gave him a bronze helmet, but it sunk so low on his face it practically covered his eyes. Saul walked up to him and handed him his scabbard and sword. David felt honored and humbled as he fastened it around his waist.

The young shepherd walked around a bit, trying unsuccessfully to get comfortable in his new attire. He felt ridiculous, and he knew he looked even worse. He could feel the amused looks and hear the quiet laughter of everyone around. Finally, he had had enough.

"I'm sorry, Your Majesty, but I can't fight with this on," he objected. Seeing the king's displeasure, he added, "It's because I'm not used to it. It will only bother me." Not wanting to give Saul time to react, he asked the attendant to quickly take it off, feeling very relieved to be back in only his clothes. He turned to face the valley where the giant was waiting.

King Saul gave the order for all the men to prepare for battle. He looked over solemnly at his commanders. "The day for war has finally come."

With his staff in his hand, the young shepherd left the king's presence and walked through the hushed soldiers who parted before him, opening a broad path for him to follow. *Everyone thinks I'm going to my death, but Lord, you'll show them otherwise.*

He saw his brothers staring at him and paused. David looked into Eliab's eyes. A lifetime of hurtful behavior flashed between them, and in an instant, David knew now was the time to let go of his anger and bitterness. He silently forgave his brothers. As he turned to continue walking, a heavy weight lifted from his shoulders. David steadied his breathing and started down the hill towards the waiting giant.

CHAPTER NINE

TWO FACES OF COURAGE

Hugo's lungs were burning. He struggled to keep up with the robbers' pace, but slowing down was not an option. His shin still hurt from the kick he had received when falling behind. He focused his attention on putting one foot in front of the other. Despite his exhaustion, he kept looking for any chance to escape, refusing to give up hope.

Stefan and Julia were hurting just as much as he was. He could hear their heavy breathing next to him, and they kept their eyes staring straight ahead.

I'm not listening to you. Hugo grew tired of rebuking his fears every few seconds. Terror threatened to overwhelm him like a dam ready to burst with too much water. *David made it sound easy. Does he struggle as much as I do?* He then remembered that the shepherd often prayed for help. Hugo shyly directed his thoughts toward heaven.

"I'm sure we'll get a lot of money for you," the robber with the ax said to Julia. He gave her a toothless smirk at the tears brimming in her eyes. "Who knows where any of you will end up? From the port in Ashkelon, you could be sent all over the world."

"We're getting too close to the Israelite army's position," the thug with the eye patch said. "We should go to the south and then come back around."

"I know what I'm doing, Gera," growled Akar. His scowl implied one more word would result in something unpleasant.

"I don't doubt you. I was only commenting." Gera lowered his head, almost bowing to Akar, but he spat in his direction when the taller robber turned his back.

Suddenly, an arrow flew out of nowhere and hit Akar in the shoulder. His shock lasted no more than a second before he grabbed his dagger. "We're under attack! Prepare to fight." He moved with such speed that no one would have guessed there was an arrow sticking out from above his left arm.

The other robbers quickly pulled out their weapons and nervously scanned the area. Whoever had attacked them wasn't in sight.

Hugo knew this was their chance.

"Help! We've been kidnapped!" he shouted at the top of his voice. "Please save us!"

The thug nearest him swung his club at his head, but Hugo ducked in time. "Run!" he hollered at Stefan and Julia. He didn't care who had shot the arrow. Nothing could be worse than these horrifying robbers.

Before anyone could move, a group of six soldiers appeared from behind nearby trees and boulders and surrounded them. They were wearing bronze armor and helmets. One had a bow, while the others held spears.

Akar let out a hair-raising scream and charged at the closest soldier. The warrior lifted his spear but realized it wouldn't be much protection against the hulk of a man flying toward him. The soldier jumped aside, letting him pass, when another arrow hit Akar in the back. He barely flinched as he turned around.

All at once, the soldiers charged. The robber with the ax shrieked as he swung his weapon at the nearest warrior, who sidestepped the attack and countered by thrusting his spear forward. He hit the robber squarely in the chest.

Two soldiers converged on another robber. He was a fierce fighter, violently swinging his club in every direction and causing the warriors to back up. Unfortunately for him, he missed making contact, and when he grew weary, the soldiers counter-attacked. They struck him with both spears at the same time.

Julia, Stefan, and Hugo huddled together for protection with their backs touching. They watched the combat in fascination and horror.

Gera observed the scene with dismay. He turned and dashed away from the battle like a spooked dog with its tail between its legs. Hugo stuck out his foot, sending the thug airborne. He shrieked as he hit the ground. Scrambling to get back on his feet, he lurched forward and disappeared around a bend.

One of the soldiers turned to go after him.

"Leave him! Why waste your energy?" yelled another of the warriors.

Akar was in a staring match with one of the soldiers, each trying to determine the best attack move. When he realized he was the last robber left, Akar made a mad dash toward the siblings and Hugo. He grabbed Hugo and, holding the boy tightly in front of him, pinned the dagger to Hugo's neck.

At first, Hugo was too shocked to react, but as his senses woke up to the gravity of his situation, an unusual calmness permeated him. It acted as a wall of protection against the panic that wanted to take over his mind.

"Don't move, or I'll kill him!" Akar roared, pressing the blade against Hugo's skin. Hugo felt a sharp, stinging sensation, and a tremor instinctively coursed through his body. A few drops of blood trickled down onto his cloak.

The soldiers froze.

"Drop your weapons!" Despite the menacing command from Akar, no one reacted. "Now!" he barked. The bow and spears were slowly lowered and hit the ground. "I'm going to walk away, and you are going to stay put!" he snarled. "If you follow me or take so much as a step, the boy dies."

Holding Hugo as a shield, Akar retreated away from the motionless soldiers, who watched with clenched fists, helpless.

Julia stood next to Stefan, and she grabbed his hand while turning to face him. Their eyes met in understanding. Lowering their heads together, they muttered a quick prayer, pleading for a miracle.

Hugo was strangely devoid of emotion as if he was having an out-of-body experience and watching the scene from above. The robber squeezed his chest with such force that it hurt.

Only you can make a move to free yourself. The thought came out of nowhere. Hugo nodded in understanding, but instantly, a fear buried deep within burst its way to the surface and flooded his heart. He felt completely helpless. At that moment, Akar jolted Hugo, breaking the terror's spell. *Don't be afraid. You can do this!*

The robber and Hugo slowly backed away from the circle of soldiers and headed down the hill. Akar couldn't see a rock protruding from the ground and hit it with his right foot, causing him to stumble and loosen his grip on Hugo.

Now!

Hugo smacked Akar in the shin with his heel as forcefully as possible. He then quickly brought back both elbows to strike the thug in the stomach.

The blows barely impacted the colossal man, like being hit with a fly swatter. Akar pressed his lips together in annoyance, but he didn't retaliate. Hugo, emboldened by his effort, kicked him again with his heel and wiggled to try to break free from his grasp. Akar's scarred face distorted into a twisted and horrifying grimace, and the veins in his neck bulged to an unnatural size. He raised his dagger just as Hugo shifted to deliver another blow with his elbow. The boy caught sight of the blade rushing toward him and ducked. The knife missed his chest but plunged into Hugo's shoulder.

Pain instantly shot through Hugo's body. Undeterred, he clenched his teeth and lifted his unaffected arm to hit Akar again. This time his strength failed him, and he harmlessly slapped the robber's torso.

The soldiers reacted at once. Picking up their weapons, they ran toward Akar and Hugo. Akar reached for the dagger lodged in Hugo's shoulder but never got the chance to grab it. An arrow flew from the raised bow of one of the soldiers and hit Akar in the neck. He let go of Hugo, who dropped to the ground like a sack full of grain. The enormous man staggered backward away from Hugo and was struck by a spear. Akar glared at the attacking soldiers in shock, then keeled over, dead.

"Hugo!" Julia flew to where he lay, Stefan right behind. She reached for the dagger.

"Don't touch him!" One of the soldiers grabbed her arm and kneeled to examine the wound. They all crowded around Hugo.

"Tell me he's going to be okay!" Julia pleaded, tears flowing freely down her cheeks. She looked at Hugo, who glanced back and gave her a weak smile.

"You were quite brave, son!" said the soldier inspecting the knife sticking out of Hugo's right shoulder. "To defy such a man takes a lot of courage."

Hugo couldn't believe what he had heard. *This is what it feels like to be brave,* Hugo thought. "I had a good example," he whispered.

"Don't speak," the soldier said. "Save your energy for the trip to camp. We need to get you there as quickly as possible."

"He's going to travel with the horrible dagger still in him?" Julia asked.

"If we take it out here, he'll bleed to death. He's losing too much blood as it is. At camp, he'll get the medical care he needs." He pointed at two soldiers. "Help him out."

They rushed to raise Hugo to his feet and locked arms to form a makeshift chair he could sit on. When he did, they slowly lifted him. Wincing from the pain, Hugo peeked at the blood trickling down his side and quickly turned away. *I'm going to be okay. I can't die in this Bible story, can I?*

The soldier who was clearly the leader faced Hugo. "Now, stay strong. It's not far."

They set off.

Hugo felt his strength seep out of him and was afraid he would pass out. The throbbing pain was getting worse. He was embarrassed he couldn't keep himself from moaning. *Don't be such a wimp.*

"Hold on!" said one of the soldiers carrying him. "We're almost there."

After about ten minutes, they reached the top of a hill and gazed at an incredible scene. Tents spread out before them as far as the eye could see. Men were sprinting in all directions as if the camp was on fire.

"How strange!" all the soldiers said at once. "What's going on?"

They hurried down the hill and asked the first man they met.

"Don't you know? Some fool has agreed to fight the giant Goliath. We're going to war!"

The soldiers looked at each other with their mouths hanging open and then at Hugo, uncertain what to do next.

"Where have you guys been?" A voice thundered above the commotion. "You were supposed to be back an hour ago." A bulky man stalked in their direction. "You need to report to the unit immediately!"

The four warriors not holding Hugo came to attention. The approaching soldier was clearly of high rank, whoever he was. "We rescued civilians from robbers," the leader exclaimed. "This boy needs medical care."

The officer glanced at Hugo with concern.

"I'm afraid you've come at the worst possible moment. We're preparing for war." He scanned the area as if looking for something and addressed the two soldiers carrying Hugo. "Bring him up there so he won't get trampled on"— he pointed to a knoll not too far away—"then go look for a medic. Good luck finding one in all this confusion. The rest of you report to your unit. Now!" He moved on.

The leader turned towards Hugo and the siblings. "May the Lord be with you." The four soldiers spun around and quickly disappeared into the crowd of warriors.

Julia and Stefan went first, followed by the soldiers holding Hugo. Their progress was slower than they would have liked because of all the activity. Some warriors almost ran smack into Hugo, but they swerved to avoid him at the last minute. Hugo felt as if his heart had jumped into his throat.

They slowly shuffled up the hill. At the top, the soldiers carefully laid Hugo down and took off to look for help. Julia almost burst into tears when he noticed how pale her friend was, but she managed to control herself.

"You can't die on us!" She brushed away a strand of hair from Hugo's brow, which suddenly felt warm.

A hint of a smile appeared on his face. "That's one command of yours I would gladly obey."

"What do you mean? I don't give commands." She glanced at Stefan with a questioning look. "Do I?"

"You can be a bit bossy at times," he smirked.

She stiffened. "Just because I have better ideas and know what we should do doesn't make me bossy."

Stefan laughed. "That's how you see it? But don't worry. We love you anyway."

Her face froze into a half-scowl, clearly unsure how to react.

Hugo watched the siblings, and a deep sadness suddenly filled his heart. He could feel himself getting weaker and lightheaded, and he knew what that meant. He desperately didn't want to cause them pain. They were his dearest friends in the whole world, but he feared he would soon be taken from them. *Not now. Not like this. Please, soldiers, come back quickly.*

"What's that monster?" Julia abruptly jerked back and pointed towards the valley.

Hugo tried to sit up to see what she was looking at, then fell back to the ground, groaning. His head was spinning. "Please help me sit up," he mumbled.

Stefan and Julia carefully propped him up against a rock.

His eyes wandered down the valley and fell on Goliath. Hugo gasped when he saw him, causing a burst of pain to course through his body, but he barely noticed since his attention was locked on the giant. Even from a distance, the Philistine terrified him. He looked like a villain who had escaped from a superhero movie. Hugo figured even the tallest NBA player would be small in comparison. He thought of the time when he got an autograph from a basketball star. He had felt so short standing next to the player, but this giant would have towered over them both.

"Look! David!" Julia pointed towards the shepherd, slowly making his way down the hill. "What's he doing?"

Stefan scratched his head. "Didn't the soldier say something about someone fighting a giant? And there happens to be one in the valley."

"Do you mean David ..." Her face drained of all color.

"Somehow, I'm not surprised," Stefan said, shaking his head.

Hugo's eyes rested on David, and he wished he could run down the hill to give the shepherd a big hug. "You see," he whispered, his face aglow with admiration, "I was courageous—thanks to you."

David paused, turned around, and looked back up the hill. He appeared to be searching for something when he caught sight of Hugo, Julia, and Stefan. His stare focused on Hugo for a few seconds. Was there concern in his eyes? David waved at them, then turned to resume his march down the hill.

"If he's going to fight that horrible giant, I'm sure he'll win," Julia declared, then crossed her arms. They watched his descent, completely spellbound.

When David reached the valley floor, he could tell Goliath wasn't paying any attention to him, probably thinking he was only a shepherd boy on an errand. David smiled to himself, grateful he wasn't wearing soldiers' gear. Goliath kept looking at the Israelite army and suppressed a yawn.

David went to the stream and picked out five smooth stones. He pressed them into his palm reassuringly and tucked them in his leather pouch before standing up. Grabbing hold of his sling, he turned around.

From up close, Goliath was even bigger than David had expected. His armor and weapons took on formidable dimensions. A wave of terror washed over David, attempting to break down his defenses and shatter his determination. *Oh no, you don't! Fear, leave me in the name of the Lord.* He inhaled deeply and closed his eyes, remembering how God had given him the victory over wild animals. When he raised his head to stare at the giant, his anxiety vanished.

David marched in the direction of the Philistine. Goliath finally took notice of him and looked upon David in puzzlement. He clearly wasn't expecting a shepherd to be the one to fight him. With his shield-bearer still in front of him, the giant trudged towards David. He leaned forward to examine David with narrowed eyes. When he straightened, he was visibly insulted. He clenched his teeth and shook with fury.

David was delighted. *You're too proud to judge me correctly, aren't you? My shepherd's clothing must be deceiving you. I bet you haven't even noticed I'm carrying a sling.*

Goliath glared at the shepherd's staff. "You come carrying a stick. Do you think I'm a dog? Do you think I'll play fetch?" He cursed David with every foul word in his vocabulary. "Come here!" he taunted. "If you think you can fight me, go right ahead! I need some exercise, and you won't even feel it when I cut your throat and give your body as food for the birds of prey and wild animals!"

David boldly stood his ground while the giant's words bounced off him. He couldn't care less about the giant's lame insults. All that mattered to him was to defend the honor of his God. He finally spoke.

"You come against me with a sword, spear, and javelin." His voice echoed off the rocks and into the ears of the Israelite army up on the hill. "Those are only weapons. I come against you in the name of the Lord Almighty. He is the creator of heaven and earth and the God of the army of Israel. You have dared to defy him, and now you must suffer the consequences." He took a step closer to the giant. "This is the day the Lord will give you to me, and I'll kill you and cut off your head!"

Goliath snorted and his mouth twisted into a scornful smirk. The shield-bearer sneered at David from behind the giant's massive shield.

David continued, unabashed. "You said you would give my body to the birds of prey and wild animals, but I tell you they'll feed on the entire Philistine army instead. Then the whole world will know the true God is in Israel!" David glanced at the Israelite soldiers looking down from the hilltop, transfixed. Smiling, he turned to face the giant and took a step forward. "The battle is the Lord's! He will give all of you into our hands!"

Goliath had heard enough. His face was beet red, and his eyes glowed angrily like tiny coals.

I've gotten under your skin, haven't I?

The giant stormed toward the shepherd, signaling the fight had begun. David's training and experience in fighting off dangerous predators took over. He dropped his staff and ran in Goliath's direction, plucking a stone from his pouch at the same time. When he was about ten feet from the giant, he came to an abrupt stop and placed the stone in his sling. He launched it straight at the Philistine's head with all his might.

By the time Goliath realized what was happening, it was too late. The stone hit him with full force in the forehead just below his helmet. A shocked look came upon his face as he fell forward and hit the ground in a loud crash. He lay there, motionless. The battle was over before it had even begun.

The shield-bearer gasped loudly. He dropped the shield and scrambled to the chariot, commanding the driver to hurry back to the Philistine army's position. On the Israelite side, the soldiers let out a loud war cry.

David, oblivious to what was happening around him, slowly approached Goliath and stood above his lifeless body. The shepherd pulled out the Philistine's enormous sword, and it took him two attempts to raise it high into the air, screaming a shout of victory. He brought the weapon down on the giant's neck. The combination of its heavy weight and extreme sharpness severed Goliath's head in one fell swoop.

When David beheaded Goliath, yells of victory and celebration from the Israelites rang out. On the opposite side of the valley, panic erupted. The Philistine soldiers started withdrawing immediately. Saul gave the order to attack, and the Israelite army, emboldened by David's victory, rushed forward, yelling as they went.

Hugo watched the soldiers run down the slope when blackness filled his vision. He couldn't hold his head up any longer and slumped forward.

"Do something," Julia yelled at Stefan, "can't you see he's dying? We can't wait for those medics." She shoved Stefan towards Hugo in anguish. Stefan turned and grabbed her in his arms because her whole body was shaking. Tears flowed down her cheeks and onto her cloak.

"Calm down, will you?" Stefan pleaded with her.

"How can I calm down? We're losing him, and you're just standing there." She tried hitting him, but he held her arms firm.

"Remember how David handles these things," he whispered in her ear. "Start praying."

"I—you're right, but I don't even know how to."

"Just talk to God, I guess."

Stefan let go of her and turned towards Hugo, who vaguely heard their conversation and was too weak to process what he had heard. The world was black, and he didn't feel any pain anymore. He had no energy left. *So this is what dying is like.*

Stefan laid Hugo on the ground. "Julia, hand me your cloak."

She promptly obeyed. With one hand, he wadded up as much of the cloak as possible while grabbing the dagger with the other. He glanced at Julia, who nodded at him wide-eyed. He yanked out the knife, flung it to the ground as if it were on fire, and then applied pressure with the cloak. To his horror, it quickly turned red. He pressed harder, but he was losing his friend! Julia stood frozen as she watched the scene.

Hugo felt his life slip away. He had no strength left. *God, I'm not ready. Please.*

When all hope left him, something extraordinary happened. At first, Hugo was sure he had died. He then realized soldiers and weapons were flying around him, going faster and faster as if caught in a massive tornado. A deafening roar followed. Hugo tried to cover his ears with his hands but couldn't move. He screamed, but the noise drowned out his shouts of terror. When it got to the point where he could no longer stand it, everything went black.

CHAPTER TEN

A New Attitude

Hugo woke up when he felt something walking on him. He opened his eyes and tried to brush away whatever it was, hitting a soft and furry object with his hand. *What in the world?* He forced his groggy eyes to focus on the offending party. When he saw what it was, he sat up with a start, causing Domino—the culprit—to leap a foot in the air. Looking around, he wondered where he was. All he could see was a tiny room lit up by a lantern hanging on the wall. Stefan and Julia were lying on the floor, taking up almost all the space.

It all came back to him in a flash—finding this room, being with David and the sheep, the robbers, the battle with the giant, and his own—*I'm alive!* He glanced down at his body. He was wearing jeans and a T-shirt, and there was no blood to be seen. *Did I dream it all?* He gingerly patted his shoulder where the injury had been but felt nothing out of place. He cocked his neck as much as he could to examine it. *My wound is gone.* Wiggling his arm up and down, he laughed. *It doesn't hurt anymore.*

He turned toward Stefan and Julia. Domino glided past him and curled up next to the girl. *It must have all been just another dream, but it felt so real.* Another thought made his heart sink. *Was David only a figment of my imagination?*

He had to have dreamt it all. There couldn't be any other logical explanation, but why had all three of them been sleeping? It didn't make sense. One doesn't doze off in the middle of the day, let alone three people at the same time on the floor of a tiny secret room. He had to get answers.

"Stefan! Julia!" he called out while standing up and stretching his legs. The siblings stirred but continued snoozing, so he leaned down to shake each in turn. Their eyes flew open.

Julia stared at the ceiling. "Where are we?" She reached out her hand to feel what was touching her and brushed up against Domino.

"At your grandpa and grandma's house, don't you remember? We found this secret room."

Stefan peered at him and sat straight up in total shock. "You're alive!"

Julia stood and covered her mouth with her hands. "There's no blood gushing out of your shoulder!"

Hugo gawked at them. "What did you say? Did you also dream about being in Israel with David?"

"You mean it wasn't real?" Stefan's eyes widened. He examined what he was wearing. "My clothes! What happened to my tunic and sandals?"

Hugo's mouth fell open. A few seconds went by before he could speak. "I have the same memory too. Stefan, you were trying to save me. Did we all have the same dream? How? It's impossible."

"Well, what exactly do you remember?" Julia asked.

They recapped the events they each had experienced and found everything matched, down to the last detail. Confused and frightened, their attention turned to the Bible on the table. The illustration of the shepherd boy with his sheep almost jumped off the page.

"He looks nothing like David," Julia said. "Too young and too scrawny."

"How do you know we saw the real David?" Hugo asked. "I mean, we can't have gone back in time and hung out with him in person. Can we?"

"Everything was so lifelike," she answered, "I think we met the real David."

Hugo visualized in his mind the David he had come to know and respect. It devastated him to think the shepherd was nothing but a dream. "Let's think this through logically. All three of us have had the same experience. So we couldn't have been dreaming, but what is the alternative?"

"That we actually time traveled to ancient Israel and met David from the Bible," Julia said.

"I don't know," Hugo said.

"It sounds so crazy," Stefan added.

"I was right before, wasn't I?" Julia shot the boys a smug look.

A light bulb went off in Hugo's mind. "I need to tell you something." He paced back and forth in the tiny space available to him. "I had two nightmares shortly before we found this room. They were so strange. In the first one, we were following David but never quite caught up to him. The second one"—he inhaled deeply—"well, the second one was us being captured by the robbers."

"Why didn't you say so before and spare us a lot of trouble?" Julia glowered at him with her hands on her hips.

"Yeah, why keep quiet?" Stefan glared at him.

"Because I didn't know what they meant. I had no idea they showed the future. I thought they were symbolic of my life. I only see it now. It's as if everything we experienced had been planned. At least, it doesn't seem to have been by accident. Man, if only we could understand what happened!" Hugo stopped pacing and leaned over the table to examine the Bible when something caught his attention. He drew closer.

"Look!" he squealed. His hand shook as he pointed to the words at the bottom of the open book. "The page ends at the exact moment in the story when we came back here." He read out loud, "And when the Philistines saw their champion was dead, they fled. And the men of Israel and of Judah arose, and shouted, and pursued the Philistines."

"So, what does it mean?" Stefan asked.

"I've no idea, but it's maybe a clue," Hugo answered. "It can't be a coincidence, can it?" All three studied the text more thoroughly.

"Yeah, you're right," Julia said. She leaned in. "See this?" Her voice quivered with excitement. "We entered the story at the exact spot of the drawing. On one side of the picture, it talks about the giant challenging Israel for forty days, and on the other side, David's father is sending him to his brothers. We made our appearance shortly before David was sent on his errand." She looked triumphantly at the boys, who examined the illustration and nodded their agreement.

"But how?" Stefan asked. "You can't just hop into a Bible story and then hop back out."

"I wish I knew." Julia crumpled her face and twirled her hair thoughtfully.

Hugo looked around the cramped surroundings carefully. "I think this room or that Bible has some strange power. Or both." His heart rate picked up.

"Do you think if we turn the page—" Julia blanched. All three stared at the Bible and then brought their gaze back to bore deep into one another's eyes. They reached out their hands simultaneously, paused, and then snapped the book shut with a bang.

"I much prefer my world, thank you very much," Hugo said.

"Imagine going back there," Julia said with a wince.

"I'd like to see David again," Stefan said.

"Enough to return to that cruel world without internet or electricity?" Hugo asked.

"And no bathrooms?" Julia said.

"And with knife-wielding thugs?" Hugo added.

Stefan shook his head. "No way. I miss David, that's all. I wish he could be here."

A forlorn expression crossed Hugo's face. "Yeah. Me too." A sadness filled his heart.

Stefan looked around. "I wonder what this room was for."

"I guess this Anna Maria used it as a place to read her Bible and pray," Julia said, "but why did she have to keep it a secret?"

Hugo scanned the room again, and his eyes were drawn to the same card he had read before their adventure began. *Hmm, that sounds familiar.* He examined it more precisely. *Yes! David spoke those exact words.* "Look!" He pointed. The siblings leaned forward while he read. "Be of good courage and he shall strengthen your heart, all ye that hope in the Lord." Hugo beamed. "David told me to be of good courage."

Julia placed her finger at the top of the entire passage. "See this? It says, 'a psalm of David.'"

They stood still with their mouths hanging open.

"You mean those songs he sang are in the Bible?" Stefan asked. "Awesome."

"He lived what he wrote, didn't he?" Hugo whispered. "He showed us how to be courageous." He gently touched the words as if he could absorb their power by tracing them with his fingers.

Julia twirled her hair forcefully. "He showed us how to trust God.

The boys nodded.

"And he faced his fears," Stefan mumbled. When he saw his sister eyeing him, puzzled, he quickly changed the subject. "So, what do we do now?"

"Should we tell Grandpa and Grandma?" Julia asked.

"Are you kidding me?" Hugo gave her a dumbfounded expression. "How are you going to explain it to them? I can hear it now. Guess what? We just spent a few days in a Bible story. How do you think they'll react to such a crazy claim?"

"Yeah, you're right. Who would ever believe us? Julia's shoulders slumped.

"No one, that's who." Hugo replied.

"We could go halfway and tell them about the room but not about what happened," she suggested.

"And risk having them get swallowed up in another story full of mortal dangers? If we hadn't left there in time, I would have died." He suddenly felt cold. "Would I have come back here?" He went pale.

Julia looked stricken, then grimaced. "I would hate to think of Grandma and Grandpa suffering in some ancient land. You're right again, which is so irritating." She gave him a sly grin.

"We can never tell anyone about what happened," Hugo insisted. "We'll look like fools." He stared at Stefan to make sure he understood. The younger boy nodded.

"You're right," Julia said. "Let's promise! Here, hold my hands."

The boys shot her a questioning look but complied and stood in a circle.

"Repeat after me: I solemnly swear to tell no one about what happened today." They repeated her words, trying not to smirk. She continued. "Otherwise, may a curse fall on me."

Stefan and Hugo let go of her hands and burst out laughing.

"What?" Julia protested.

"You're ridiculous," Hugo said with a chuckle.

"Okay, then. How about this? So help me, God."

"Better," Hugo conceded. They again grabbed each other's hands and repeated the words.

"Okay. We've given our word. Our secret is safe," Julia said with an air of gravity.

As amused as Hugo was by this little ceremony, he was nonetheless satisfied that they had vowed to keep quiet. If word ever got out, all three of them would look like fools.

Julia suddenly looked worried. "We better close this room before Grandma and Grandpa come back. I don't want them to catch us in here." She very carefully returned the Bible to the center of the table. Domino rubbed up against her, and she took him in her arms.

Hugo grabbed the lantern. They all paused briefly before crawling under the desk to enter the bedroom. The boys then pushed the desk out of the way. Once free from its barrier, the secret door slammed shut.

They dragged the desk back to its original location and stacked the pile of papers on top of it, hoping everything looked as it had before. He checked to make sure the little cat figurine was standing up straight. "We'll have to tape it down to make sure Domino doesn't move it again."

"I don't know why, but I'm sad." Julia walked back to the wooden panels and touched the secret door, her fingers following the contour of the carved animals.

"Yeah, it's as if we slammed the door shut in a friend's face," Stefan muttered.

Hugo inexplicably felt as if they had cut themselves off from something supernatural and significant. He tried to shrug it off, but the nagging feeling wouldn't disappear.

Domino rubbed against Hugo, who absent-mindedly picked him up.

"I thought you were allergic." Julia leaned over to pet her cat, wiggling in the boy's arms to get free.

Hugo felt as though someone had punched him in the stomach. He quickly handed Domino to her and avoided eye contact, but he could feel her questioning stare. *If David can admit his errors, then so can I.* "I lied." His heartbeat sped up.

"But why?"

Do I dare? David would. "Because I was afraid of Domino."

"That's it? You're hardly the only one, you know." She turned to head out of the room.

Hugo watched her go. It had never occurred to him that others could also be scared of Domino, and he breathed a sigh of relief. He followed Stefan into the corridor full of sunlight streaming in from the open bedroom doors. When they reached the siblings' room, Julia faced Stefan. "You should move to another room."

"Really?" He cocked his head at her defiantly. "So you're giving orders again, aren't you? Well, you can forget it." He stormed away.

Julia closed her eyes for a second. "I'm sorry. Let me start again. I like this bedroom. Could you please choose another one?" She exhaled. "If you want, I'll move."

Stefan smiled. "If you put it that way, I'll find another spot."

They heard a door open and close downstairs.

"Your grandparents are back. Whew! We got out of there just in time," Hugo said.

They rushed down the stairs.

"Grandma! Grandpa!" Julia wrapped her arms around her grandparents and squeezed as hard as she could, holding them trapped for a few seconds. When she let go, they took a step back and examined her, perplexed.

"We've only been gone since this morning," Grandma said. "Why the joyful greeting?" A beaming smile nonetheless formed on her face.

Julia hesitated. "Um, aren't you happy I'm happy to see you?

"Of course, I am."

It didn't take long for the grandparents to invite Hugo to dinner. An hour later, everyone sat around the table, enjoying Grandma's famous shepherd pie. *This is nothing like shepherd's food.* Hugo thought back on his meals with David and was surprised to find he missed them. *Could I even find figs if I wanted?*

Once everyone sat back with full stomachs, Julia finally broached the subject Hugo had hoped she'd raise.

"Who was our ancestor, Anna Maria?" She tried to appear as casual as possible by pouring another glass of iced tea.

Grandma raised an eyebrow. "I don't know much about her, to be honest," she said. "She built this house with her husband. I think his name was Henryk."

Julia looked over at Stefan triumphantly, "I told you so." She then turned back towards her grandparents. "What else can you say about her?"

Grandma paused for a second as if trying to remember the stories she had heard in her childhood. "Family tradition says she was a good woman everyone liked, but Henryk was a stern and difficult man."

"In what way?" asked Stefan, sitting up straight.

"I don't remember details, I'm afraid. They had three children, and she died in childbirth. That's all I know. Why are you asking?"

"Oh, no reason." The siblings looked away. "We saw her name scribbled somewhere," Julia muttered.

"Really? Where?"

"Somewhere upstairs. Forget it." With those words, Julia stood up to clear the table.

Grandma eyed each of the kids suspiciously, but she didn't press the matter further.

Once the meal was over, the siblings accompanied Hugo to the front door. They stepped outside with him, making sure to close the door behind them.

"I guess this Henryk guy didn't want his wife to read the Bible," Julia said.

"Yeah. I imagine her hiding in the tiny room, reading and praying, while Henryk had no idea what she was doing."

"Do you think he ever suspected she had a hiding place?" Stefan asked.

"Who knows? There are so many secrets I would like to uncover," Julia said. "But, they're probably buried forever."

"Maybe not. You never know." Hugo's eyes twinkled.

For the rest of the summer, Hugo hung out with Julia and Stefan as much as possible, but the end of August barreled down on them like a runaway freight train. Before they knew it, the day of the siblings' departure back home was upon them.

Hugo took twice the usual time to reach the siblings' house. Dragging his feet, he walked up the steps and knocked at the door, which opened instantly.

"Where have you been?" Julia gave him an accusing look. Her eyes were red and watery.

"We've been waiting forever." Stefan ran over and slapped Hugo on the shoulder.

Grandpa and Grandma took this as a cue to leave the three alone and promptly marched out into the kitchen.

A tall, blonde woman Hugo had never seen before came down the stairs. "Hi, Hugo. I'm Julia and Stefan's mom. I've heard so much about you."

Hugo shook her hand. After a few minutes of small talk, Mom headed toward the kitchen. "I'll finish packing the car."

"Do you have to leave so soon?" Hugo asked once she was gone.

"We tried to change her mind, but she wouldn't budge." Julia said.

"You'll come to visit, as you promised?" Stefan asked. "Won't you?"

"Of course," Hugo answered. He shuffled his feet and stared at his shoes. "There's something you should know." He hesitated. He couldn't seem to get the words he wanted to say past his throat until he thought of David. *I'm not shrinking back anymore.* He swallowed hard. "You two have become like a brother and sister to me. I love you so much and will miss both of you!"

Julia and Stefan came up to him and embraced him. "We love you, too!" they said in unison.

Mom walked into the room. "Um, I'm afraid everything is ready." She grimaced and left.

"Call us anytime, okay? And we can always reminisce about David," Julia said.

"Remember the snake?" Stefan laughed. Hugo joined him, but Julia wasn't amused.

"Not funny. I could have had a heart attack." Her words caused the boys to howl even harder.

Hugo accompanied Julia and Stefan to the car, where they hugged some more. As he watched them drive away, an emptiness engulfed his heart. His only comfort was knowing their friendship would endure.

On the way home, Hugo caught sight of Sammy's house at the end of the street, and his stomach churned. Ever since *the day*, he had avoided any contact with Sammy, but he was done running. His adventure with David had ignited a growing conviction to make things right. As much as he dreaded it, he knew what to do.

He marched past his home all the way to Sammy's house. The closer he got, the faster his pulse raced. *God, I need your help, okay?*

While debating whether to knock on the door or wait outside, he saw Sammy walking with his dog. Without hesitation, Hugo headed straight for the boy as if his legs had decided to take off on their own.

Sammy noticed him and did a double take. He stopped in his tracks and pulled on the leash, forcing his unhappy Sheltie to stop sniffing at the nearest bush and sit by his master.

Hugo couldn't tell if Sammy was shocked or upset. "Hey," he said.

"Hey."

Silence.

"Sammy, I'm sorry"—his voice cracked—"for abandoning you to those monsters. You were so brave." He shuffled his feet. "And I wasn't." Hugo was strangely numb like a giant vacuum had sucked up all his emotions.

Sammy examined him without saying a word, but soon a sympathetic smile illuminated his face. "No problem."

"I—I know I did wrong, and I admire you for standing up to those thugs. From now on, I want to be different."

Sammy remained quiet, but his smile widened from ear to ear.

Hugo ran out of words to say. "See you around."

"Yeah, take care."

While strolling home, Hugo's body felt like it had just run a marathon, but his spirit was as lightweight as the butterflies fluttering around his garden. He'd accomplished mission number one, but he knew his biggest test was still to come.

Two days later, on the first day of school, Hugo left home with a pounding heart. Despite his best efforts to stay calm, a river of sweat poured down his back. At this rate, he would be soaking wet when he got there.

"Wait!" Sammy trotted to a stop next to him.

Hugo smiled. "How ya doing? Ready for the new year?"

"You bet."

They talked about the Phillies' chances for the playoffs until they reached the school. Once in the hallway, Hugo glanced around with apprehension, but the bullies were nowhere in sight.

The morning flew by uneventfully, but lunchtime loomed ahead.

While waiting in the cafeteria line, Hugo spotted Dan entering the dining room, and his heartbeat spiked. He took a deep breath. *Stick to your plan. You can do this.*

Once he got his food, he headed for an empty table. He placed his tray down and grabbed the chair when he felt a presence next to him. It could only be one person. Hugo sent God an urgent plea for help and turned to face the bully.

Dan sneered and flashed him a wicked smile. "Hi, Hugo, remember me?"

Hugo remained quiet.

"You know the drill." His voice was low. "Just leave the tray and walk away."

"No." Hugo sat down, grabbed the fork, and took a bite of the mystery meat on his plate.

Dan's eyes widened to the point of showing more white than brown. He clenched and unclenched his hands. "As you wish. But the whole school will find out about how you ran like a sissy and left poor Sammy behind."

Hugo had rehearsed his answer countless times. "If you give too many details, you'll only incriminate yourself. But if you spread an anonymous rumor, it will sound like fake news. So go ahead." He took another bite. "By the way, have you seen Sammy's father? He's a karate champion or something. I wouldn't want to be in your shoes if he ever discovered the truth."

Hugo honestly had no idea how Sammy's father would react, but a little speculation couldn't hurt.

Dan's eyes narrowed. "You want to play hardball? Fine by me. I'll see you after class." He smirked and strutted away with his two cronies in tow.

Hugo couldn't concentrate on any of his remaining subjects, and he couldn't even take notes. He thought about David facing Goliath. The shepherd must have been terrified, right? After all, he had admitted to being afraid, but he also didn't listen to the lies his fears told him. And he trusted God.

When the final bell rang, Hugo didn't rush outside like the rest of the students but took his time to leave the building. He plodded along the sidewalk until he got to the shortcut he usually took, which bordered an empty field and a patch of trees—where *the day* had happened. He knew the bullies would be waiting for him. Should he take the long way and avoid them? *No. Let's get this over with.*

He advanced about twenty yards, stopped, and waited for the bullies to come to him—the encounter would happen on his terms. Sure enough, Dan and his sidekicks didn't take long to appear from among the trees. They swaggered up to him.

Hugo watched them approach. *Uh, God, I need your help and strength. Now!*

"So, you want to play the rebel?" Dan sneered. "We're going to have to teach you a little lesson."

He swung for Hugo's head, who ducked in time, causing Dan to plunge forward and almost crash to the ground. He whipped around and glared at Hugo.

Dylan grabbed Hugo from behind. "Just try to duck now, you sissy," he hissed into Hugo's ear.

Hugo thought about Akar's grip, and Dylan was no Akar. He lifted his right leg and forcefully struck Dylan in the shin with his heel.

"Ow!" Dylan let go of Hugo and grabbed his leg.

A cheer erupted from a distance. Hugo and the bullies whirled in the direction of the shouts and saw about ten teenagers gaping at them from the sidewalk.

Hugo had hoped for spectators, and their presence boosted his confidence. "You can beat me up all you want," he focused on Dan's shocked face, "but I'm done cowering before you." He stood as tall as he could manage and folded his arms. Part of him wanted to bolt to join the onlookers, but something told him he should stay and be the last to leave.

Dan didn't say a word, but his lips curled into a sneer, and his cheeks became mottled. "This isn't over." He stomped off toward the trees with Dylan and Mark scurrying behind him to catch up.

Hugo strode toward the group of teens, which had grown to about twenty.

"Way to go, Hugo!"

"Great kick."

"You showed them."

Not knowing what to say, Hugo remained silent but was sure he had a stupid smile on his face. He knew he didn't deserve the praise. Like David, he had experienced help from above. *Thank you, God.*

Despite Dan's threats, he and his cronies never bothered Hugo again, not seriously anyway. They threw insults his way occasionally, but their words harmlessly missed their target. Hugo's fame spread throughout the school, and he became a hero to all the bullies' other victims. From then on, he never had problems making friends.

In the months that followed, Hugo thought about David, especially when taking Gibson for walks through the lush countryside behind his house. He came to see his adventure as proof of everything being under God's care, but he gave up trying to analyze and understand exactly what had happened. No explanation made sense. He eventually came to accept and embrace the experience with his heart, deciding that certain things are best seen through the eyes of faith.

END OF BOOK ONE

ABOUT THE AUTHOR

Carol Schlorff has always felt like an outsider. She was born in North Africa to American parents and grew up in France. At age fifteen, her family abruptly moved to the Philadelphia area due to her mother's deteriorating health. Adjusting to American life while attending high school was a dreadful experience.

After graduating from Penn State, Carol joined the Army in search of adventure. She was stationed in exotic—for her—locations like California, Arizona, and Texas. When her time of service was up, she headed off to Chicago to spend a year at Moody Bible Institute to brush up on her biblical knowledge.

Since then, Carol has been living in Cracow, Poland, where she teaches English, organizes English language camps, and writes a blog on all faith-related topics (at bibleandsoul.com).

Carol enjoys taking care of her cat, Tabasco, visiting new places, watching a good murder mystery, and getting nervous while rooting for the Philadelphia Eagles.

A NOTE TO MY READERS

Dear Reader,

Thank you for reading *How to Kill a Giant*. I hope you found it both fun and inspiring—if that's the case, I've accomplished my purpose for writing the story.

The idea for the book came from a desire to illustrate the life-changing power of the Bible. I also wanted to dispel the unwarranted notion that the Scriptures are boring. How can the Bible be snooze-inducing with such colorful characters as David on its pages?

Could you do me a favor and post a review on Amazon or another favorite website? (Be honest, of course.) Your opinion is vital in helping readers pick out a book, and the more reviews, the better. Thanks for your help.

On the pages that follow, you'll find an excerpt of *How to Make a Miracle*, Book Two in the *How to Be a Hero* Trilogy. The threesome of Hugo, Julia, and Stefan finds itself back in the ancient world, smack in the middle of a new—and more deadly—adventure.

Please consider signing up for my newsletter to stay up to date with future publishing dates and bonus materials. Don't worry. I won't fill up your inbox. You'll only hear from me when I have newsworthy information to share. You can sign up on my website: https://carolschlorff.com

Finally, feel free to email me with your comments or questions at carol@carolschlorff.com. I would love to hear from you.

Blessings,

Carol

HOW TO MAKE A
MIRACLE
BOOK TWO OF THE HOW TO BE A
HERO SERIES

PROLOGUE

Nasiya could tell something was wrong. A flock of birds shrieked as they took flight and fluttered away. She nervously scanned the hillside near the field where her beloved lamb was blissfully grazing. She squeezed her eyes and scrunched her face to listen with all her might for any unusual noise. A shiver crawled up and down her spine when she heard footsteps in the distance. *I better hide.* She hurried towards her sheep while desperately looking around for shelter.

Too late. Stomping feet echoed off the rocks, and a terrifying sight appeared before her eyes. A dozen prisoners in chains trudged forward, surrounded by warriors brandishing swords and spears.

"Nasiya, run!"

She recognized the voice of Miss Sarah, her neighbor. Instantly, she sprinted towards the hillside but could hear scampering behind her that rapidly drew nearer. She jumped over a rock and zigzagged between some bushes. Whoever was behind her stumbled, then cursed. Elated, she spun her legs even faster while a tiny flicker of hope that she might get away gave her the strength to keep going.

Nasiya ran as fast as she could, but she was abruptly picked up right off the ground and thrown over a shoulder like a sack full of barley. She pounded the back of her attacker with her fists. "Let me go! You have no right." She tried to kick the man, but he held her too tightly, and she couldn't move her legs. "I said, 'Let me go!'"

The soldier remained silent as he marched her back to the others. He then threw her to the ground.

"Ouch! Be careful," she yelled and rubbed her sore leg and knee.

"You better be quiet for your own sake, or you may not live to regret it. Now stand up."

Nasiya hesitated and was rewarded with a bonk to the head. She jumped to her feet, and the soldier tied her hands together with rope. He then pushed her in the direction of the other prisoners. She looked around for her lamb and saw it standing, untouched, in the far corner of the field, eyes wide with terror. *At least she's okay.* "Run home," she whispered. Her eyes filled with tears.

"Move it," another man screamed, and the group set out.

Nasiya furtively eyed the other prisoners. They were all from her village. Mr. Jesse, who sold eggs to her parents, shuffled closer. He nodded at her with eyes full of tenderness and sadness. A gash on his forehead caused a stream of red to run down his face and neck, onto his cloak, and all the way to his legs, finally reaching his sandals.

"You're bleeding," Nasiya said. She tried to touch the blood flow with her hands, but he grabbed her arm to stop her.

"I'm okay. It's nothing."

"It don't look like nothing."

"Quiet!" A soldier bolted towards them and shoved Mr. Jesse to the side, almost knocking him over. "No talking. The next person to say a word will have a personal encounter with my sword." He touched the weapon's handle and looked around, scrutinizing all the prisoners. He smirked while his eyes shone with an evil glare.

Nasiya bit her lips to keep quiet. Anger boiled inside her to the point where she was sure she would burst. She concentrated on putting one foot in front of the other to control her temper.

They marched nonstop for so long that Nasiya's legs felt like they would fall off. Miss Sarah stumbled and came crashing to the ground. She lay motionless for a few seconds, trying to catch her breath. The nearest soldier kicked her in the ribs and pulled her to her feet by her hair. The poor woman moaned. She swayed from side to side as if about to topple over. Nasiya and another prisoner dashed towards her, and together, they helped her regain her balance. They resumed their march.

No one dared slow down after that.

They stopped for the night and set out again at first sight of dawn. Nasiya focused all her energy on keeping the pace the soldiers had set. She lost track of time and was no longer sure how many days went by. As they advanced, more captives were added to their group.

The sun was setting when they reached the outskirts of a town. The first people they passed ignored them completely as if the sight of prisoners was no big deal. Nasiya had no idea where they were, but she was sure of one thing—they were no longer in Israel.

They came to a large stone house surrounded by a walled courtyard. The soldiers directed them into the enclosure, then closed the heavy wooden gate behind them. Finally, they could rest! Nasiya threw herself to the ground, convinced that she would never have the strength to get up again. The other prisoners collapsed just as eagerly all around her. Fortunately, none of the soldiers paid them any attention.

"I—"

"Shhh!" Mr. Jesse leaned in towards Nasiya as he held his finger over his mouth.

The girl nodded and remained silent.

The soldiers busied themselves with setting up camp for the night. As in the previous evenings, they weren't in a hurry to provide food or water for their prisoners. Nasiya's mouth felt as dry as the Negev Desert, and she had difficulty swallowing.

The other captives sat still, not saying a word, as fear and despair flickered in their eyes. Many had bruises, and some, like Mr. Jesse, were covered with blood, some of which had dried.

Suddenly, the sound of horses' hooves filled the air and loud voices reverberated outside the courtyard. The soldiers hurried to open the gate. Three men on horseback rode in.

"Everyone, stand up! Don't you know whose presence you're in?"

The prisoners groaned as they rose to their feet, but no one dared to disobey.

Nasiya observed the three newcomers transfixed, especially the man whose elaborate bronze armor reflected the setting sun, making him appear to be glowing. He wore a helmet, and an enormous sword hung from his side.

"I see you have a good catch this time," he said with a smile and dismounted in one smooth motion.

One of the soldiers rushed to take hold of the reins. "The gods have been good to us."

"I'm here to review the merchandise before you take it to market." He pointed towards the prisoners. "I have a need to fill."

"As you wish, my Lord."

A growing sense of dread filled Nasiya's mind as the man approached the captives and walked from side to side in front of them, sizing them up. He paused before her, and she felt like a waterskin had burst in her heart. He moved on.

Whew!

"I'll take the young girl," he said as he marched back toward his horse.

It took a second for his words to register. "No!" Nasiya yelled out in terror. Her lungs stopped working, and she started gasping for air.

"Shut up!" The soldier closest to her slapped her face with such force that she crumpled to the ground.

"Stop!" The man in the armor took a few steps in her direction. Was there compassion in his stare? Impossible. "Don't worry. You'll serve my wife. You won't find a better situation." He then spun around on his heels and hurried away.

Mr. Jesse rushed to help Nasiya get back on her feet. "If the man's telling the truth, you'll be okay," he whispered.

The girl stared at him and took a few deep breaths. The despair she was feeling flashed across her eyes. "Has the Lord abandoned us?"

"No way. He'll be with you. Don't give up hope."

"What about you?"

Mr. Jesse gave her a mournful smile. At that moment, a soldier grabbed Nasiya's arm and dragged her toward one of the other newcomers. He lifted her high and plopped her down on the horse in front of the rider. The man put his arms around her to keep her from falling.

"Don't say a word, and don't move." He spurred the horse, who took off in a gallop.

Nasiya would have slid right off had he not been holding her. The longer the horse ran, the more she felt all emotion vacate her body, as if she was stuck between a dream and reality. She wished she could open her eyes to find herself back in her bed, staring at the loving face of her mom. But there was no waking up.

Made in the USA
Monee, IL
14 July 2023

39087188R00096